Oceans of Longing

OCEANS OF LONGING

Nine Stories

SITOR SITUMORANG

Translated by

HARRY AVELING
KEITH FOULCHER
BRIAN RUSSELL ROBERTS

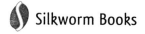 Silkworm Books

ISBN: 978-616-215-149-1

This edition is published in 2018 by
Silkworm Books
430/58 Soi Ratchaphruek, M. 7, T. Mae Hia, A. Mueang Chiang Mai, Thailand 50100
info@silkwormbooks.com
http://www.silkwormbooks.com

Cover: Photo by Jim Beaudoin on Unsplash
Back cover: Painting of Sitor Situmorang by Misbach Tamrin, based on a photo from the 1950s
Typeset in Adobe Garamond Pro 12 pt. by Silk Type

Printed and bound in Thailand by O. S. Printing House, Bangkok

5 4 3 2 1

CONTENTS

PREFACE

Sitor Situmorang (1924–2014) was one of the greatest and most prolific Indonesian poets of the twentieth century. A recent edition of his collected poetry covers almost a thousand pages. He also published a collection of three plays and wrote a small number of short stories, about twenty-three in all, which were widely admired. As a master of the newly emerging national language, he further made his mark from time to time by translating such authors as John Wyndham, John Galsworthy, William Saroyan, Dorothy Sayers, Arthur Rimbaud, Rabindranath Tagore, and Eduard Hoornik.

Sitor's poetry has been translated into many languages, including English, French, Dutch, Chinese, Italian, German, Japanese, and Russian. Through Silkworm Books, his complete short stories are now available for the first time in English: *Oceans of Longing* contains nine thematically related stories, while a second collection, *Red Gerberas*, contains the other fourteen.

Oceans of Longing is a collaborative work. The idea behind this volume first arose in discussions among Keith Foulcher, Brian Russell Roberts, and Harry Aveling. At Sitor's request, Harry had been working on translating the complete short stories, while Keith and Brian had just completed *Indonesian Notebook: A Sourcebook on Richard Wright and the Bandung Conference* (Duke University Press, 2016), a study of Wright's visit to Indonesia in 1955. In *Indonesian Notebook*, they had traced personal, literary, and political interactions between this prominent African American novelist and his Indonesian hosts, including innovators of Indonesian literary and aesthetic modernism such as Sutan Takdir Alisjahbana, Mochtar Lubis, Asrul Sani, Achdiat Karta Mihardja, Siti Nuraini, and Sitor Situmorang. Collaboration on a collection of Sitor's stories, particularly those he was working on during the early to mid-1950s, seemed like a rewarding next step.

Oceans of Longing is based on Sitor's prize-winning 1956 collection, *Pertempuran dan Saldju di Paris* ("Combat" and "Snow in Paris," the names of two of the stories in the collection). The six stories from *Pertempuran dan Saldju di Paris* are supplemented by one thematically related story from *Pangeran: Kumpulan Tjerita-Pendek* (Lord: A collection of short stories, 1963) and two from *Danau Toba: Sekumpulan Cerita Pendek* (Lake Toba: A collection of short stories, 1981). We have checked and compared different versions of the individual stories published in Indonesian periodicals and other collections of Sitor's work. At times we have made corrections when mistakes have clearly crept in. At other times we have needed to use our own judgment as to which version to privilege. For instance, the 1955 publication of "Combat" in the literary magazine *Siasat* included a 300-word introduction that was omitted, perhaps for aesthetic reasons, when Sitor published his 1956 collection. However, we have opted to restore this introduction, following the text of J. J. Rizal's definitive anthology of Sitor's short stories, *Ibu Pergi ke Surga* (Komunitas Bambu, 2011), which Sitor himself carefully supervised.

Our aim has been to produce a collection of good-quality stories that contemporary readers can enjoy. *Oceans of Longing* is also intended to be useful to students of Indonesian culture and literature as well as to those who study international modernism and the conditions of modernity across the planet.

The order of the stories here moves, as Sitor himself did in the early 1950s, between Amsterdam, Paris, and Indonesia, back and forth, to give the collection a sense of divided consciousness, imitating a mind in Europe having flashbacks to Indonesia, or a mind in Indonesia having flashbacks to Europe. The Indonesian stories constantly remind the reader that even when Sitor is in Europe, his stories come out of Indonesia and, even more specifically, from the region around Lake Toba in North Sumatra where he was born and raised.

The work of translation was shared equally among the three translators. We each took charge of three stories. These are signed at the end with the name of the translator responsible for the first draft and final version of that story. But we also read and commented on one another's work, benefiting from each other's suggestions and insights. The nine stories are, in that sense, joint translations as well.

Brian is in Provo, Utah, while Harry and Keith are in Melbourne and Sydney respectively. We worked electronically—translating, discussing, commenting, and sharing resources. During our work, various problems presented themselves. The first and most important was the fundamental question of the style of the translation. We wanted to capture Sitor's own voice, not making it too colloquial but certainly not making it too formal or literal either. Sometimes we had to choose between American and British terms for the same object (what are the differences between a "bathrobe" and a "dressing gown"?). Larger cultural issues emerged from time to time. For example, the conclusions of Indonesian short stories sometimes aim to produce certain effects on Indonesian audiences that a literal translation will not typically convey to a reader in English. In a few instances, we engaged in a type of cultural translation, departing from the source texts in terms of pacing or nuance, in ways that attempt to offer English-language readers something that approaches the effect that the Indonesian stories might convey to Indonesian readers.

There was also the question of a title for the book. This collection overlaps with Sitor's 1956 collection, but the two are not identical, so a simple translation of the 1956 title did not seem right. Instead, we arrived at a new title adapted from one of Sitor's poems, reflecting Sitor's enduring and existential attachments to his region and traditions of origin, even as his international and intellectual travels drew him into wider cosmopolitan currents. In his poem "Pulau di atas Pulau" ("Island on an Island"), Sitor calls the Toba region, and particularly the island of Samosir, "the starting point for all my wanderings" and the existential ground for "an ocean of longing." His piercing stories bear out this perpetual tension between the urge to wander and a longing for origins.

We have benefited from the comments of several friends. Tiffany Tsao has been a long-term ally of the project and gave insightful comments on a handful of the stories. Michael van Langenberg (a scholar of North Sumatran political history) read the collection's longest story, "Combat," and assured us that he could hear "Sitor's voice telling the tale," that the translation "caught his voice perfectly." Fahri Muhammad Shihab consulted with Brian on early translation drafts, and Scarlett Lindsay, editor for Brigham Young University's Faculty Publishing Service, read through the manuscript and commented with great insight on each of the stories. We are grateful for their support.

Finally, it needs to be said that we have learned from working together that there are, in fact, no "final versions"—just versions "torn from our hands" and sent to the publisher. We would like to thank Trasvin Jittidecharak for putting her trust in us and Joel Akins for his careful reading and attention to detail.

Harry Aveling
Keith Foulcher
Brian Russell Roberts

Sitor in Italy in the 1950s.

Sitor at home in Leiden, the Netherlands, in 1982.
Photo by Barbara Brouwer.

Sitor in Harian Boho in 2007. Photo by Barbara Brouwer.

Sitor at a seminar in honor of his 85th birthday, held at Erasmus Huis,
the Dutch cultural center in Jakarta. Far left: Guruh Sukarnoputra,
youngest son of former president Sukarno; right: Nikolaos van Dam,
ambassador of the Kingdom of the Netherlands.
Photo by Barbara Brouwer.

I

OLD TIGER

T he bus disappeared into the forest a few hundred meters from where I stood. As far as the eye could see in the direction I was heading, to the south, there was only wild grassland rippling in the cold wind. It was still early, and as usual during the dry season, the air was clear. The sandy clay of the cracked road sparkled with morning dew.

I looked around. There was no one in sight, no one to meet me as my father's letter had promised. But these days, who would be willing to climb way up here out of the valley unless there was a hefty payment involved? It used to be that an old man living alone, abandoned by sons who had gone off to seek their fortunes and by a wife who preferred to die sooner rather than later, had a right to call on the assistance of any young person. Our traditions of mutual aid would have made this quite normal. And then there was the simple question of respect for our elders.

At this time of year, there would always be a few workers tending to the road. They would have come from the valley to work for wages after a meager harvest so they could at least have enough money to go to the store, or to pay taxes, or to buy clothing once a year.

But there was no one to be seen.

Suddenly my gaze fastened on a cone-shaped hut that had previously been imperceptible among the tall grass. A thin trail of smoke rose above it into the cold, bright air.

A sign of human presence.

Carrying my suitcase, I made my way in that direction with a sense of relief. The silence of the field, broken only by the wind whistling through the gulf between heaven and earth, brought on an empty feeling, an intense urge to seek the company of some other being, as if to share in the oppression of a sky that seemed far too vast.

I hesitated a moment in front of the hut's "door," a burlap curtain. If there's anyone inside they're sure to have heard my footsteps, I thought, and they should be giving some sort of sign that they have been waiting for me since the bus passed through. Any sign of life amid the silence of this high country should be a reason to rejoice. But there was no sign of life other than the thin line of smoke. So I bent down and peered into the hut's darkness.

Someone was there.

After my eyes had adjusted to the darkness I saw an old man wrapped in a blanket, ensconced by the fire and warming himself in its flickering glow. He turned his wrinkled face in my direction and gazed at me with sharp eyes. He didn't say a word.

Feeling let down and rather frightened, I asked, "Excuse me, sir, has anyone come from the valley?"

He stoked the fire by scratching the coals with a dry branch. Cold air blew into the hut through the sieve of dry grass walls.

The man moved a bit and said, "Were you planning on being met? Maybe they got the day wrong. Stay the night. Maybe he'll come tomorrow."

Then he was quiet. "Stay the night?" I wondered to myself. But then I realized that twenty-four hours in this place meant nothing more than a sunset and a sunrise, connected by a night. Time here was flat as a field and endless as the empty sky. At certain times, a person feels hungry, so he eats. And the days go by according to the nightly moonrises, with nights becoming the beginnings of new days.

Maybe I was the one who made the mistake in naming the day I would arrive, because I had forgotten their way of counting days.

For an ordinary person, walking alone down the steep path into the valley was half a day's journey. It was very dangerous. A foot could slip and a person could fall into a deep ravine. There would be nothing to slow his fall, because, as was the case on the high plateau itself, the downward slopes and adjacent ridges only supported weeds. And there would be no one around to help.

I placed my suitcase in the corner and sat close to the old man, who meanwhile had set a clay pot on the stove. He was cooking rice. There was grilled dried fish to go with it.

I wanted to ask many questions. For example, was he a workman? And what about life in the valley during the fifteen years since I had left? Where was he from? No one lived for tens of kilometers in any direction on the west side of the great Lake Toba.

But the old man didn't seem to want to talk. So I offered him a cigarette and turned to leave the hut. He took the cigarette in his rough-skinned hand and then began munching at one end, crushing it to a red pulp that looked like a newly opened wound. It was so red—the color of the betel he chewed. He crushed the other end of the cigarette, still clean and white, between his hairy black fingers. I went outside, leaving him in the hut.

That night after eating for the second time he left the hut, humming softly as if the sound came from deep within him. When he stood I saw his straight, broad chest. He slung the blanket over his shoulders, stooping as he made his exit, and then disappeared into the darkness outside.

Because there was no lamp, I spread out the blanket from my suitcase and settled down to sleep. I had stopped ruminating on the quiet old man's temperament and now waited patiently for tomorrow.

The evening dew descended, creeping into the hut, and from far away in the jungle I could hear the whooping of a troupe of orangutans signaling that night was advancing.

Where had he gone? I wondered about this during the final seconds before I fell asleep, and I felt as if I were sleeping on a carpet of soft earth that floated in the heavens, close to the stars, so close they could be picked like fruit in a field. Then I smelled the scent of the soil, which filled every vein in my body. I died, melting into the earth—such were my dreams.

Morning light streamed through the grass walls. With a fleeting feeling of confusion I looked around and felt the earth where I had been lying. Then I remembered my actual situation. But the old man wasn't there. I saw only a spear propped up in the corner, and I smelled fresh meat. I got up and went out.

The old man was warming himself up in the morning light. He was cooking some kind of tea in a clay pot that was set on the fireplace he seemed to have put together just for this purpose. He warmed his hands by the fire.

His hands were covered in splatters of coagulated blood.

"Where were you last night, sir? Didn't you sleep?" I asked, speaking in the respectful tones we use with older people.

"Oh, an old man like me doesn't need to sleep much anymore."

"What did you do all night long?"

He was quiet, looking in the direction of the sun as it rose from the edge of the field on the east side of the valley. With squinting eyes, he seemed to wish his gaze could pierce the sun's very center.

"Son, when I was young I was a coward."

I silently awaited what he had to tell, thinking it might shed some light on all the things I had been wondering about since last night. At least that was my hunch as I watched him hesitate before continuing.

"When I was young, we often came up here to work on this road, not long after it was opened up. Three or four of us, usually. It added to our income.

"Do you see that hill over to the southeast?" he said while pointing to the place he meant. "That's where we dug the tiger trap. Because where there are tigers, there are no wild pigs, and wild pigs were what we were after." He was quiet again.

"Once, a big tiger got caught in the trap. But when the four of us went to kill it, the tiger sprang out of the pit with all the strength it could muster and broke through the covering on top. Turns out the covering was too weak. And it went for me."

The old man parted his blanket to show his left foot. Just a stump. Then he pulled the blanket closed again.

"Drink," he said, offering tea in a coconut shell. "I didn't marry— no one wanted me. I couldn't even work. All I could do was cook rice for friends who *could* work.

"Last night I killed it," he said with a strong light in his eyes.

"The tiger?" I asked.

"Yes, of course," he said.

"But isn't your story from a long time ago?"

"Sure, but I know I'm right. I'm sure it was him. There's only one tiger in this area. And I've always known him. I know his stripes, and the look in his eyes.

"All night long I waited above the trap. And he came along, smelling the wild boar meat I had placed at the bottom of the pit as bait. Then he entered.

"I waited for sunrise. He stared at me. He recognized me and growled quietly as if to ask forgiveness. Then I thrust my spear into his haunches.

"He didn't even roar. It was as if he felt the blow was only fair. Yes, yes . . . I felt the same way, and it seemed he had been waiting for this for decades."

The old man lowered his head and blew on the fire, as if the mountain wind weren't enough.

"Look at the skin hanging inside the hut," he said.

I was quiet. From far away, the echoing noise of whooping orangutans welcomed the new day.

The old man stood up, stretching his arms and puffing out his chest. He leaned against a crutch he held under his left arm.

"Go ahead and pack. You don't want to keep your father waiting.

"If we leave early like this, we'll be able to get to the valley just before nightfall," he said as he looked toward a left foot that didn't exist.

So we packed and I didn't say anything else. I was thinking of the legends about these sorts of things that I had heard as a child.

"Your father is dead. It was me who got your letter," he said after we began to walk.

Translated by Brian Russell Roberts

2

MOTHER GOES TO HEAVEN

Mother finally died after suffering tuberculosis for barely a year. She was sixty-five and her dry old body could no longer withstand the damage done by the germs that ran wild in her lungs. It was impossible to buy medicine; there was never enough food in our village far away in the mountains, and certainly not the proper care she needed. When she died I said to myself, "Thank God!" The old woman had suffered a great deal.

Purely by chance, I was there when she died. Over the preceding few months, I had twice been summoned by telegram: "Mother very ill. Come." I came the first time. She quickly revived. "See," someone said consolingly, "you're getting better. You're just missing your children!" In fact, she was ready to die. I could tell from the expression on her face. Like my father, who was much older than she was, Mother had nothing more to live for. We—her two sons— had both gone away to find work. The large house was empty. The fields were neglected. My mother and father only needed to tend a small portion to meet their own needs. They wandered around inside the house as if they were in a large grave, as she herself said. No one ever visited them. What would visitors talk about with a garrulous old man and his almost-dead wife?

I received the second telegram. But I didn't go. For some reason I decided that she would live another six months. So I sent her a jacket instead. Mother sent a letter to my oldest son, which she had dictated to someone else because she was illiterate. The letter said, "Your grandfather is jealous, please send him a woolen jacket like the one you sent me!" The request was confirmed by my father's thumbprint. I sent the jacket.

Then the third telegram arrived. Some sort of intuition ordered me to return home. When I arrived in the village alone, my father said resentfully, "Have you come on your own?"

For many years no one had known where my younger brother lived.

As we ate that night, Father asked, "Have you quarreled with your wife?" Then he grumbled and went outside. "It's expensive, Father!" I said. But he disappeared into the darkness after saying: "When your mother dies, I won't live very long after that, and I've never seen my grandchildren!"

Mother just smiled.

The next day, after observing my mother, I decided that she wasn't about to die. I slightly resented coming in response to the telegram. I was almost ready to return to my work on Java but I stayed. By chance, it was close to the New Year, meaning close to Christmas as well. I knew my mother liked having me close to her at Christmas, although my father didn't. I don't think he ever knew the significance of his having been baptized as a Christian forty years ago. He still recited magical spells when something unusual happened to him or his family. If a tiger took one of his water buffalo on an open plain in the mountains, he would recite mantras and burn twigs at night. The greedy tiger would die! He was convinced of that.

Mother was different. Not only did she not believe in superstitions, she faithfully attended church meetings and was a prominent member of the congregation when most of the population were still pagans. Of course, she was famous for the medicines she made too, but she did not chant spells over them— she just spat into the mixtures.

When Father went to church, he had a special seat near the minister, on a large chair facing the congregation, because he was a raja and had been even before the Dutch government and the missionaries arrived. That was his right, and each time he went to church he sat in his chair, dozing until the service was over.

On the second day I was home, the minister came to visit. Because Mother could not attend church on Christmas Eve, the congregation would celebrate Christmas at our house! Mother agreed, nodding as if this were perfectly natural.

I felt uneasy for some reason but said nothing. In fact, the Sunday service had already been celebrated at our house several times. It almost seemed as though this would be a sort of a funeral. I remembered the sermons of my childhood. The foolish stares of the congregation and Father's dozing. The harsh, discordant singing and the strong odor of sweat on people's bodies. The time spent talking outside in the churchyard after the service had finished. I didn't see these things in that way when I was a child. For a child, the churchyard was full of marvels. The leafy candlenut tree, the garden of fruit trees—rose apples, jackfruit, and mangoes—and the many sugarcane bushes in the minister's yard. On Christmas Eve, I always received the leftover candles. That was my special right, and the children all allowed me to have them.

When he was about to leave, the minister invited me to follow him to his house. Because there was nothing else to do in such a lonely mountain valley, I went. Anyway, I wanted to see the old church, which I hadn't visited since I left the associated primary school some twenty years ago.

The road to the church passed through the village and the vegetable gardens. The minister asked, "Why didn't you come to church when you were here a few months ago? You stayed for over a week, didn't you?"

I avoided his question by asking this and that about various people in the village. He asked me how things were on Java, about Jakarta, the possibility of war over Formosa. How long would the current cabinet last? I answered without much enthusiasm. Finally, we reached the churchyard. My first impression was one of amazement. The church and the minister's house were much smaller than I remembered. The yard was not as large as it had once seemed. The candlenut tree was not as tall, neither was the steeple of the church, nor the rooster made of thin metal, which showed the direction of the wind. Nothing had changed. The old wooden church was exactly the same. It was very dilapidated. We entered the church, which was still being used as a school, except that now there were even more benches, as well as a small temporary shed to one side of the main building.

The church and the shed held three hundred pupils and four teachers. "One of the teachers has a certificate!" the minister proudly told me.

The walls of the church were covered with children's drawings. I looked at them and high up saw a picture of a buffalo defending its master from a tiger. My picture.

The minister's wife called out. She had prepared coffee. "Just a minute!" the minister replied and his voice echoed against the hills surrounding the valley. After he had closed the door of the church, his dog came and licked at my feet: the eternal silence.

As he sipped his coffee, the minister said politely, "I'd like you to read the gospel on Christmas Eve. It would make your mother very happy if you did."

As I looked at a torn picture of the head of Jesus hanging on the cross, I said, "I'd rather not, pastor. One of the elders should do it."

"The elders are organizing the congregation, lighting the candles, singing the hymns, looking after the school children. They are leading the choir. We are going to sing your mother's favorite hymn, 'In the Hands of God!'"

I didn't like it but I didn't say anything. The minister apparently considered that a sign of acceptance.

"They are preparing cakes for the children too. Sihotang has made a generous donation. Do you still remember him?"

I returned home, feeling empty inside myself. I imagined the people gathered in our house. Where would we put Mother? She couldn't sit up for very long. Could she lie down, perhaps?

When I arrived home, I found her squatting alone on the floor of the middle room, preparing a drink from the condensed milk I had brought with me.

Christmas Eve arrived. Father had dressed in clean clothes early in the day. He sat alone in one corner of the large inner room, pounding his betel nut in a silver mortar.

Two girls I did not recognize dressed Mother and placed her on a wooden bench, then moved her some distance away from Father. The Christmas tree from the forest had already been prepared and set in a corner. The candles had not yet been lit.

After Mother had been made comfortable, the two girls left. They wanted to get ready as well. The ceremony would begin in another hour's time, I estimated. I went to my room and sat in a chair, letting my thoughts drift about. From time to time Mother coughed, the sound cutting across the hiss of the kerosene lantern.

My reverie continued for perhaps half an hour, I wasn't sure. When I became conscious again, I realized that I couldn't hear Mother coughing. Neither could I hear Father's grinding. He must have been chewing the pulp in his toothless mouth. The sound of the lamp was louder than before. I came out from my room, looked briefly at Father, and then at Mother's figure stretched out under a cloth on the bench. "She is sleeping," I thought. Then I approached her. I examined her face, with her sunken eyes and hollow cheeks. Then her chest.

"Like the breast of a chicken," I thought. Suddenly I realized that her chest was not moving. I touched her forehead, then opened one of her eyelids. She was dead. A strange sense of gratitude blocked the feelings that filled my throat. I looked toward Father. He didn't know anything. How could I tell him? People would be coming for the service soon. I covered her face with the cloth and before long heard people arriving. The minister, the elders, and the congregation entered, taking their places on the floor, sitting cross-legged in tight rows, first of all in the corners, and then when the corners were filled, reluctantly scattering out toward the center of the room.

"Is your mother asleep?" the minister asked as he handed me the Bible.

"Yes," I replied.

"Good! When we come to her favorite hymn, we can wake her up," he said.

He began to organize the congregation. The elders carried out their various tasks. Finally the whole room was full, except for a small space around Father. The schoolchildren sat near Mother's bench, with their backs to her, facing the Christmas tree in the corner. The colored candles were lit and children gasped in wonder and delight. I stood rigid near the wooden bench with the Bible in my hand, feeling awkward, like a new priest about to give his first sermon.

The service began with prayer. Father continued grinding his betel nut. Then the hymns. Then it was time for the reading of the gospel. Was that my voice? The congregation continued singing. I lost all sense of time but I could hear a droning sound: "*When Jesus was born in Bethlehem in the land of Judea . . .*"

Bowing low, the minister politely took a few steps toward me in order to tell me to wake up Mother. "We're about to sing her favorite hymn!"

I nodded and he went to conduct the choir. Before they began singing, he threw a glance in my direction and I responded with another nod. The choir began "In the Hands of God!" I couldn't catch the words. It was a hymn I had never known, and the children near the bench were restless and talked a lot to each other. I saw that Father had stopped pounding betel nut and was staring dazedly at the bright Christmas tree.

The minister prayed, "Almighty, most Merciful God, we hold our mother up before You. Life and death are in Your hands. May You receive her into heaven!"

After singing "Silent Night" and offering the closing prayer, the service was almost over. The cakes were cut, the drinks shared. The minister and the elders sat near Father. Then, as he passed through the crowd in the center of the room, the minister cheerfully called out in Mother's direction, "Sleep, Mother, you don't need to have any cake, just sleep!" I went to my room and put the Bible on a table, then came out again, peering around, looking at people.

"Come and sit over here, sir," said an old man. "Let's talk. What news do you bring from Jakarta?"

I excused myself and left the house. "Let them find out for themselves," I thought. After some time, I peered back into the house again. It appeared that no one had bothered to disturb Mother as she lay sleeping. Nor did they until there was no one left.

After they had all gone, I told Father that Mother had passed away. He stopped grinding his betel nut for a moment, and said, "Call your uncle!"

Before leaving, I extinguished the candles.

A few days later, after Mother had been buried with both traditional and Christian rites, Father called me over to him.

He was standing in a corner of the vast yard and gestured to me to follow him. I didn't know what he wanted. Once I was close, he said, "Do you have any money?"

I was startled because I didn't know the purpose behind his question, but finally I said, "How much do you need?"

"A thousand, two thousand rupiah, should be enough," he said.

"For what?" I asked, following him to the edge of the yard. He put his hand on my shoulder and, looking at the lake down below, said, "I want to be buried here. You have to make me a fine cement grave. When I die, I want you to move your mother here too."

I could only ask, "Why here?"

Father took his left hand from my shoulder. He turned to look toward the peaks of the mountains and said, "From here I can see both the high plains and the lake."

I said nothing.

The lake sparkled in the midday sunlight. Father walked away and left me. I saw the minister approaching.

The minister came toward me, and when he reached me he said, "I hear you're leaving tomorrow. I hope you have a safe journey."

Then: "Please don't be sad! You can see how much the villagers and her kinsfolk loved and respected her. She is now with the Lord."

"Yes," I said.

"Yes, I know that you believe, even though educated people don't like coming to church these days. I never doubt that you still have faith in Christ." It was as if he were talking to himself.

"Isn't that right, sir? How could anyone not believe in God? How could there not be a heaven?" His face was like that of a goat facing the chopping block.

"You're right, pastor," I said. "Of course there is a heaven." Then the minister left me.

I walked toward the Christmas tree lying dry and neglected in the yard.

With a single match, I lit the tree and it burned like a bonfire, just as when I was a child. The ashes scattered across the yard and spread in the wind toward the blue lake below me.

Translated by Harry Aveling

3

THE DJINN

I

On mornings like this, the air drew its light from within the clear lake. And the sun in the silken sky warmed itself on the same morning air, an atmosphere echoing with thousands of otherworldly voices conjoined in a whisper.

The wind wasn't blowing by the lakeshore. But the tall grass rustled with the hidden movement of a snake. The droning of a beetle. Then the silence was filled with the vibrations of dragonfly wings, a pulse hovering above the horizon.

Lying on his back in the grass, Aman Doang stared at the sky but saw nothing. He thought but wasn't aware of anything. He was spellbound like nature itself, as if the whole world were waiting for something to break the calm.

Aman Doang stood, went to the edge of the water, and washed his face. For a moment he looked at his reflection in the surface of the lake. Then his eyes were drawn to a school of fish that hung suspended, motionless in the water.

After a moment, he looked away, turning his gaze toward the other side of the bay.

There were echoes of laughter from the bald mountain several hundred meters across the bay, as young women worked at cutting thatch. They were melancholy echoes, like soft ripples that flowed from the other side. Aman Doang turned and looked behind him, where rice paddies rose one after another like stairs and the village lay scattered across the valley.

The path toward the center of the village traversed a cemetery. Aman Doang let his eyes rest on it for a minute. Reverberating cries filled the air, bouncing off the valley walls toward the mountain slope that flanked the bay. They weakened into a sweetly coaxing murmur, until finally they were no more than a whisper disappearing far into the bottom of the lake, settling into the sediment.

The echoes disappeared—far, far, beyond help, irretrievable, into the kingdom of Boru Saniang Naga, the goddess of the lake who lives in that underwater world. It is a place no humans can venture, except as victims of the storms that always ravage the surface of the lake during the dry season, when the wind hits the water from atop the mountain, rolling like a giant stone, shaking the lake into waves as high as houses. In the maelstroms, the fishermen's slender boats capsize and are sucked into the underworld, never to return. The locals set out in their boats, searching for the lost fishermen, striking a gong so the dead can find their way back to this world. But Boru Saniang Naga only sets their corpses free, shackling their spirits as ransom for the sins of humankind.

Oh beautiful and maleficent water goddess!

This was the fate of the spirit of Saulina, Aman Doang's younger sister, who had never been set free. After a day and night of searching for her to the steady beat of the gong, all they found was her body.

Aman Doang had been sitting in the village square repairing his hoe while his baby son crawled around nearby. Then, out of nowhere came a scream of pain. How could Aman Doang have known his younger sister was in danger in the bushes behind the village wall? How could he have known that the village chief would unleash his lusts upon the honor of his little sister—such a sweet child—and that she would throw herself into the lake before either Aman Doang or anyone else knew what was happening?

Boru Saniang Naga returned only her corpse. The village chief was fired and punished with three months in jail. Nothing more, since Aman Doang's family was only a recent addition to the village community.

He began walking toward the village but there were a few villagers sitting in the path through the cemetery, blocking his way. He took a different path, through the bushes and bamboo, and along the top of the village walls, entering his home from behind. This is how it would be from now on. Wherever he went Aman Doang would carry the burden of shame.

That evening, Aman Doang's eyes met those of his elderly father in the dimness of the house. The old man said nothing, and Aman Doang turned away. Lost in his own thoughts, he gazed at the bright moonlight that came in through the gaps in the thatched roof.

Later that night, after eating, and after everyone else had gone to sleep, Aman Doang crept out of the village and headed for the rice fields.

Before leaving the house, he said, "I'm just going to open the ditches to let water into the fields." But there was no one to hear, because everyone was asleep. His father coughed but still slept soundly.

Aman Doang pulled a knife from a gap in the boards of the house and sharpened it on a river stone. As he walked toward the fields, the moon appeared in the sky. Then it disappeared. And then the moon shone again. Its intermittent light sliced the air above the lake. The black mountain hovered nearby. The snorting of water buffalo came from behind the village wall.

When Aman Doang returned to the village, the air was bright with moonlight, which filled the yards and reached even into the spaces beneath the houses. He made his way toward the village chief's house. It was raised on stilts, and underneath were six water buffalo. They were skittish and restless, bumping their horns against the beams supporting the house. "Who's there?" called a person from inside the house. Aman Doang was silent. Through the gaps between the floorboards he could see an oil lamp being lit, and then there was a movement toward the door. Aman Doang saw someone's feet. As they descended the steps, he recognized the former village chief's sarong. The chief stopped for a moment, as if to listen. The only sound was the grating of bamboo canes rubbing against each other in the wind. Otherwise all was quiet. Aman Doang leaped from his place of ambush and strangled him. Aman Doang picked up his fallen knife and went home. He slept soundly beside his father.

The next morning they found the village chief dead, next to a lamp that had run out of oil. The villagers were quiet after seeing the corpse and avoided Aman Doang's gaze when he too came to see. Aman Doang's father heard that the village chief was dead but he didn't go to look. Instead, he went to the lakeshore without a word, mumbling to himself.

Aman Doang said nothing during the trial and remained silent when the verdict was read out: Twenty years in prison! He would be sent off to Java and from there to the prison island of Nusakambangan!

On the day he was to be transported by police-boat to the jail on the far southern shore of the lake, from where he would be continuing on to Java, all of his relatives accompanied him. Before he boarded the motorboat he was permitted to shake hands with them, though his own hands remained shackled. That morning, people saw an extraordinary light in his eyes when his mother embraced him and Aman Doang looked toward the mountain peak, his gaze moving past those of the onlookers and rising above their heads, fixed on a point somewhere on the horizon. People said they were no longer the eyes of a human but those of the djinn that now resided in his body. When they shook his hand, it felt as though they were shaking the hand of a dead man. No one ever came back from Nusakambangan!

His father didn't come to see him off.

He had only appeared once during the trial, taking the chance to shake his son's hand and whisper in his ear before he was put back into his cell.

"Eat! Eat!" said the old woman as if trying to cheer up a little child. Aman Doang's mother tried to get him to eat some rice cooked in the village. But her son had no appetite for food.

For the past several days, everything had smelled to him like a corpse. He no longer knew the difference between day and night. During daylight hours it was as if the sun hadn't risen but rather stayed on the horizon, while at night the moon hung firmly in the middle of the firmament without giving light, like the eye of a dead fish. Nights passed very quickly. He had only just been escorted back into his cell in the late afternoon, and it was already morning again. Aman Doang hadn't slept at all. A thousand beetles buzzed in his head. In his mind's eye, his footsteps were light—only the chain was heavy, but even that floated on the lake water. And someone was singing, calling to him, weeping. Boru Saniang Naga!

Look at the face of that woman. Is that my wife? No, no, that's a djinn, carrying a dead baby!

Thousands of hands reached for him, but he collapsed and tumbled into a deep ravine. Like a chunk of stone that had no grounding, plunging ever deeper and filling the air with a great roar. Then the church bell tolled, signaling someone's death: clang . . . clang . . . clang . . .

The motorboat started up. Women were crying. But there were no tears from his father.

"I left the knife where you would find it!" his father had whispered in the courtroom. "May God protect you."

Human voices disappeared. The motorboat was now just a small speck on the vast expanse of water.

* * * *

People never return from Nusakambangan. Has it already been fifteen or seventeen years that he's been gone? Who remembers him apart from the very old? For a long time now, his wife has been able to laugh again, even though her face is always grim, unmoved and showing no sign of either joy or sadness.

II

After fifteen years confined in the prison on the island of Nusakambangan, Aman Doang came home. His sentence had been remitted on the birthday of the queen of the Netherlands, his punishment cut short. For fifteen years he had neither sent nor received news from his family. What had there been to tell? He was counted among the dead, in his own eyes and in the eyes of the family he had left behind. It was only when his mother and then father died that he received word.

But here was his son, already sixteen years old. And he found that his wife had remarried.

Aman Doang was dead.

Upon returning he intended to become a barber. It was something he had learned in prison. But who would want their hair cut by an ex-convict? Many stories arose about his ferocity in prison, where the guards had selected him as an enforcer, someone to keep other inmates in line. "He was so good at being cruel that he got out early!" they said.

For some reason, it wasn't long after he returned before there arose the story of late-night visits to the valley by a dragon-snake. No one had ever seen it. But at night, people could hear something that rent the water and the air, a sound that resonated like the collapse of a mountain.

And another old story was told about a pair of shepherds—brother and sister—who met with divine punishment for falling in love. They turned to stone at the precise second they embraced.

People would step aside when Aman Doang passed by, avoiding his eyes.

Then after some time out of view, Aman Doang returned one day from the far side of the lake with a boat and fishing gear. After that he was seldom seen in places the people frequented but rather spent his days and nights fishing by the lakeshore, far from human habitation. Along the lakeshore, where rocks abounded, there were lots of caves that fishermen used as sleeping quarters or places to take shelter.

After Aman Doang became a fisherman, the other fishermen abandoned all the caves. And finally, Aman Doang didn't return to the village at all. But his boat could still be seen at night when he was catching fish. Someone reported that he finally made a permanent home in a big cave near the mountainous stone that jutted out into the lake and was considered sacred.

On bright days when the water was very clear, the big stone was visible down into the depths of the water as far as the eye could see. Down that far, all kinds of big fish appeared. But no one dared catch them. If people passed through this area at all, they didn't row quickly with their oars but went slowly, warily so as not to trouble the water and disturb the gods.

In this way, Aman Doang lived in complete isolation for many years.

It was said that he had married the water goddess, Boru Saniang Naga, who provided him with food and permitted him to catch the fish of the sacred stone.

Until one night there was no light from the cave. From that time on, people no longer saw the fire that had usually shone bright from afar like a torch flickering in the night.

The people who lived in the valley were restless. They were frightened, and there were some who said that the gods were angry and must be placated. It was decided that they would hold a ceremony offering up a sacrifice to redeem the souls of Aman Doang and his younger sister Saulina.

So one day the old and young people of the valley boarded several large boats and, while sounding the gongs, headed toward Aman Doang's cave. All this was overseen by a shaman who stood at the head of the foremost boat, banishing all the djinns that guarded the way to Aman Doang's cave. Upon arriving, they saw only a swatch of cloth from an old sarong in the fire pit, and fish bones.

"He's been taken by Boru Saniang Naga!" said the shaman while reciting an incantation and sprinkling the cave with lime juice. Then a white chicken was ceremonially killed.

The djinns departed from the cave. The souls of Aman Doang and Saulina were calmed, and by order of Boru Saniang Naga they became occupants of the sacred stone.

For a long time after that, there were no more incidents of people drowning in the lake or killing themselves by plunging down into its waters.

Translated by Brian Russell Roberts

4

The Last Supper

I

It was after three in the morning as our Land Rover snaked along the steep and winding road toward Prapat on the edge of Lake Toba. In the shadowy light of the waning moon, the large island in the middle of the lake lay stretched out like a sleeping giant. The town of Prapat, on its narrow peninsula and with its twinkling lights merging with the moonlight on the surface of the lake, looked like an oceangoing ship tied up in port.

With no sense of excitement or happiness, I felt a surge of recognition: the land of my birth!

Near the stall that sold Padang food at all hours of the day and night there were a few big trucks piled high with latex from the rubber plantations down south. They were awaiting their drivers and crewmen, who were inside warming themselves with plates of steaming rice, their dark bodies wrapped in thick jackets. They were heading for the coast, on the border between Aceh and East Sumatra, where the smuggling and bartering operations with Penang and Singapore took place. They transported the latex from the area around Pekanbaru, a thousand kilometers away, not in line with any laws of economic behavior but following the twisting paths of the illegal trading networks, like these nighttime roads heading down to the lake.

"Tires sell for 40,000 rupiah these days," someone said to no one in particular.

I wondered how much it would cost to hire one of these trucks, and what they might bring back from the smuggling operations down on the coast.

My older brother, who was driving the Land Rover we'd borrowed in Medan, ran a trucking business himself. And while we ate, he talked prices with the other drivers and ended up asking one of them for a jerry can of fuel.

I knew we still had our own supply of fuel, but since we had to circle around the southern shore of the lake to reach our village on the western side, we needed as much as we could find. During the rest of the trip, especially in the hours before dawn, we were unlikely to see anyone and there would be nowhere to buy fuel once we left the open fields and were swallowed up by the forests. All through the night on the trip via Prapat my brother hadn't wanted to talk. He put all his concentration into the driving, belting along as though we were trying to chase down someone up ahead. It had been that way since we'd left Medan the night before.

It was nearly five in the morning before we finally ran into something that slowed us down. In the dim light of the moon, a group of women were pounding pandanus leaves on the asphalt surface of the road. At another point we were forced to reduce speed for a silent procession of farmers, each carrying a tool of some kind as they headed out into the fields. Neither of us spoke, but the same shadow hovered above both of us: Father's face!

"Will we get there before he dies?" The question hummed in the air around us. Judging by his jawbone and the stumps of his teeth, the doctors estimated Father's age to be 113. In the last few years, the "old age" ceremony had been performed for him on three separate occasions because he felt his life was almost over, but still he went on living.

This time I wasn't coming for another ceremony. Rather, I was there because my brother had made a special trip to come and get me, saying, "Father has suffered a lot. He's worn out. It's time he went to his eternal rest. But he won't go until he's seen you one last time."

After he'd settled on the purchase of a truck, we left Jakarta for Sumatra.

Just before dawn, we reached the highest part of the plateau with its broad open fields. In the first rays of the morning sun the fields shone with a golden light, made even brighter by a layer of sparkling dew.

"Where are the herds of wild horses?" I wondered. The neighing of horses out in the fields grew stronger in my memory, awakening that old symbol of the freedom of the open fields and the unbridled spirit of the mountain skies. We'd covered tens of kilometers, but there wasn't a single horse to be seen anywhere now. Times had changed. The unsealed roads still lacked asphalt, but they were now covered with a layer of stones.

Horses, lake, forest, steep hills thrusting into the skies, dark-skinned people who count the centuries by generations and measure suffering against happiness, people who make sacrifices for their offspring and know love by the quality of the mud in their rice fields. Among them was my father, determined not to die before he saw me again!

We stopped at a settlement in a clearing in the forest, and I was introduced to the people living there. It turned out we were distantly related, descended from the same ancestors. Family! Blood relatives. Welcome! I gave one of the children a ball from the stock I'd bought as presents for the children of relatives in the village.

"How is Father?" my brother asked them.

"We haven't heard," they said.

"But it's a good thing he's come," someone said, looking in my direction.

Back in the forest we came upon a truck loaded with timber, but there was no one around. My brother blew the horn of the Land Rover to let them know we were there, and from somewhere in the forest came the sound of axes in reply. We moved on without comment.

A moment later, my brother said, "That was what's-his-name's truck." Like the sound of ships signaling to each other in a fog, we could hear music calling people home.

"Father's still all right," my brother said.

"How do you know?" I asked.

"That truck wouldn't be up on the mountain if something had happened to him," he replied.

"All over the island and out to the west they're making preparations for Father's party." What he meant by "party" was the funeral, the burial ceremony after Father passed away.

"They've planned festivities over four days and four nights. No one can justify seven days and nights anymore," he said. "Four days will be enough to allow family to come from all over the Batak lands. They've set up a telephone chain and a message system so the news of Father's passing reaches people quickly."

As we came down into the valley where the lake meets the shore, we saw some villagers carrying firewood and blocks of timber.

"They're the stall holders getting ready to build the temporary shelters. It'll be like a big night bazaar, with thousands of visitors from all over."

II

"Now I've got all six of you here before me," Father said that night after dinner. The words were translated for us by my younger brother, who could read the movements of Father's toothless gums. Anything you wanted to convey to him had to be shouted loudly and slowly into his ear, because his hearing wasn't good anymore either.

We formed a half circle in front of him, six brothers sitting cross-legged before our father, awaiting his words.

"This is the first time I've had you all here," he spoke again, referring to my presence. "I'm going to hold a feast for you all. So you'll need to get one of our ancestors' buffalo from up on the mountain."

The six of us looked at each other, aware of the solemnity of his words but immediately also thinking of the practicalities of fulfilling Father's wishes. "How are we going to catch a wild buffalo in the forests up on the mountain, with less than twenty-four hours to do it in?" That was the question that needed answering, and it seemed as though all of us were wondering the same thing. The buffalo Father was referring to were a herd of a few dozen wild buffalo, all that were left of the hundreds he had inherited from his forebears. Catching one of them when there were festivities to be organized or when a working buffalo was needed was not easy, and usually took several days. First it was a matter of finding them in the forests, then singling out the right kind of animal for the particular purpose. A working buffalo had to be taken alive, and one for a feast had to be shot.

Father had made it clear that the feast was to be held on the following day.

"What if we make it the day after tomorrow?" my eldest brother suggested. When the question was conveyed to Father, he just replied, "I said tomorrow." And then he asked to be put to bed again, because he was tired.

The next morning, Father smoked the cigar I had brought and drank the milk my wife had sent from Jakarta. As happened every day, people came from near and far, some of them bringing offerings of food as though asking for blessings from a holy man. He received them all, touching the offerings as a sign of acceptance, though he didn't eat anything. They put babies in his lap for him to bless, and smiling with pleasure he stroked their little heads.

He asked one of the old women for a boiled egg, and someone else for a bottle of sulphur water. A third person he asked for some limes to perfume his bathwater. All these requests were fulfilled. They ran off to their own villages, overjoyed to be answering Father's last requests. It was only later that I learned that their happiness was due to Father's generosity. He was giving them the opportunity to offer him something that was within their means, without the need to mount expensive ceremonies. They were too poor for that.

Late in the afternoon there were celebratory shouts mingled with the noise of the Land Rover on the mountain slopes. They'd succeeded in shooting a young female buffalo in accordance with Father's wishes. This was the sacrifice needed for the last supper he wanted to hold with us, his sons. The head of the hunting party proudly reported the successful outcome to Father, only to be on the receiving end of a retort from the bed where Father was resting. "Who said you wouldn't be able to do it? You people just don't have any faith." Then he went back to sleep.

A little later, after the ceremonial food was ready, they woke him up. The seven different parts of the buffalo's head had been chopped up and mixed with its blood: the tongue, ears, brain, flesh, skin, bone, and eyes. The heart was cooked whole.

"The food is ready, Grandfather," called my brother's daughter, the girl who took care of him on a daily basis. They helped him sit up, and once he was propped up against the wall with his pillows he moved his hand in a circular motion from left to right, as though checking who was present. "Are you all here?" he asked.

"Yes, Father," said my oldest brother, now a grandfather himself.

"Where's the buffalo's heart?" he asked. One of his granddaughters passed him the plate with the steaming heart on it. His favorite sharp knife lay beside it.

"Now cut the heart into six pieces," he told her, touching the hot meat. His granddaughter cut the heart as he had asked.

"It's ready, Grandfather," she said. He reached for the plate and took a piece of meat.

"Come, each of you," he summoned us, and we each stepped forward to receive a slice of the sacrificial heart. My oldest brother went first, then the second, third, and so on. I was fifth in line.

Father waited for us all to finish the food he had given us. "Now you have eaten food from my hand. The six of you are my blood. To you I say"—he spoke slowly, like a minister conducting a church service—"to you I say: From my ancestors to my grandfather and my own father, I have been taught: Love your fellow man, especially your own brothers; stand together and look out for one another. Support each other, and stay united; be of the same mind and bear one another's burdens.

"Sometimes there will be someone younger or poorer than yourselves who is worthy of imitation. When that happens, make that person an example of how you yourself should act. These are my words to you," he said, signaling that he wanted to lie down again.

Everyone present was overcome by what had just occurred. "It's just like in the holy scriptures," commented the minister. He looked relieved, probably because he had concluded that there was nothing in Father's ceremony that bore any trace of the old superstitions, as he had originally feared might happen.

The feast proceeded as a joyous occasion, marked by conversation, happy laughter, and a spirit of peace and harmony. When night fell, Father asked my brother to call the *kecapi* players and get them to play his favorite songs. They played the old songs, but in the modern style. This made Father angry. He asked to be moved into a sitting position, then said he wanted to go to sleep. The *kecapi* players felt guilty and began to play the old songs in the original style. When Father heard them, he nodded with pleasure. Suddenly he asked them to stop playing and raised his head as though he were about to speak to the company again. And so it was. "Tomorrow I . . . want to perform the prayers to the gods of Pusuk Buhit!" he announced.

Everyone was shocked. Praying to the gods of Pusuk Buhit, the sacred mountain, was the high point of the heathen rituals, and it was strongly condemned by the church. Prayers to the gods of Pusuk Buhit!

"Call the *gondang* group from Limbong," Father said. They were the renowned ceremonial *gondang* performers who were considered the only group able to play the music for the ritual veneration of the Holy Mountain.

Like all his requests or instructions, this pronouncement held mystical authority over the people around him, and even though they had difficulty suppressing their religious concerns, they did as he had ordered. That night, I received a special summons to sit beside his bed. There was something else he wanted to say. "The day after tomorrow, go home. Go. I know you've got a lot to do."

The following night, after the ceremonial *gondang* players arrived, everything was prepared for the prayers to the mountain. The minister had asked people to try to get Father to back down, but it was to no avail. The ceremony, which I'd heard about but never actually experienced, was both very solemn and very unnerving, like all the pagan rites.

The sacrifice was a goat, cooked according to the ancient ritual as an offering to the gods. Father forbade the use of pork.

During the ceremony, every single flame and lamp in the village had to be extinguished. No one was allowed to cross their yard or even go in and out of the house. Once the fires and lamps had been extinguished in the late afternoon, all the doors and windows had to be tightly closed. Everyone was aware that the ceremony was going to take place, and no one dared step outside.

At precisely seven o'clock in the evening, the drumbeats began, a sound that was even more terrifying in the darkness because of the mystical power the ceremonial music embodied. Dressed in the clothes that marked his status as a Batak chief, Father was raised to a standing position. He lifted a platter bearing the sacrificial meat, ready for the esoteric prayers—a meeting and a union with the spirits of the ancestors there on the summit of Pusuk Buhit, beyond the reach of earthly eyes, sensations, and words.

Very early the next morning I took leave of Father as he lay stretched out on his bed. Since the night before, he'd seemed somehow very distant from us. I moved very close to him to make my farewell and spoke right into his ear, "Father, I'm leaving now."

He nodded and then drifted back to sleep. I took a shortcut to the lake road. Arrangements had been made for a boat to pick me up in the bay of the valley where I had been born. It would take me to Prapat, from where I could take a bus to Medan.

When the boat reached the open waters of the bay I looked back toward the valley sleeping in the dim light of dawn. To the right I could clearly make out the peak of Pusuk Buhit, rising into a gray-blue sky. Lighting a cigarette to ward off the cold, it occurred to me that in my whole life Father had never once initiated a conversation with me or spoken directly to me. All except the night before last, when he bid me farewell with the words, "The day after tomorrow, go home. Go. I know you've got a lot to do."

Translated by Keith Foulcher

5

A JUNIOR DIPLOMAT

W hen he thought about how his life had turned out, as he was doing right now, sitting behind a big desk in a quiet office at around ten in the morning with no new work to do, he would often break into an unconscious smile. It was a smile of satisfaction, but one cut by mocking lines that blurred the contours of his mouth.

He was well aware that the time would come when he would reluctantly have to give up the life of a diplomat, a junior diplomat, living here in Europe, in a country that was as orderly as he liked to keep his office space. It would be difficult to leave his job behind, and not just because he would miss his comfortable livelihood. In fact it wasn't simply comfortable—sometimes he thought "lavish" would be a better way to describe it. But!

But . . . there was something else as well. When he began thinking about it, he would normally start flipping through the neat stack of papers that sat before him. Life suited him here, because he was someone who liked order, ranging from small things, like well-kept files, the placement of his pens and pencils, and the clothes he wore, to "big" things, like respect for his superiors, most importantly respect toward His Excellency the Honorable Ambassador. And of course respect for his subordinates, ranging from the guard at the door, to the messenger boy, to the local European staff, and so on, according to their variously tiered ranks.

In short, he might make mistakes in his nonprofessional life, but with regard to office matters and relations among personnel— these he would not and, finally, could not ignore. Because!

Because, if he didn't behave in this way, he didn't deserve to be a public servant—being a public servant requires that one follow a certain morality. This he knew. In this, he was already well seasoned. It had not burdened him that this particular morality required attitudes that were different from those normally found outside the community of public servants—that is, it hadn't burdened him after a certain amount of time on the job. However.

However, there was always something that disquieted him when he felt he needed to rationalize to himself any particular action he had undertaken in the realm of public service.

Consider his experience last night with Madam Murdono, a woman who had come here as part of a parliamentary entourage. This was the woman who, in Indonesia, had taken it upon herself to eradicate prostitution! And her trip to Europe was purely in pursuit of that noble endeavor.

Imagine him—an attaché!—being asked to provide a detailed report on local prostitution: its social circumstances, hygiene measures taken by the country's government, and more, all the way down to the going rates and such like things. Did she think this was a fit task for a diplomat? He had a right to be angry. Actually, she hadn't come right out with it, like the other Indonesian visitors, whose first request after they sorted out their hotels and other basic arrangements was always something like, "Hey, man, show us all the really hot spots, will you?"

Guests would usually make these requests with a smile that floated somewhere between embarrassment and the mischievous smirk of a university student, even though at home these people were highly respected senior members of the community.

He had so much experience in this regard that now he could immediately identify people's inclinations upon first meeting. This usually happened when he was picking up guests at the airport, watching them emerge from the planes dressed in warm clothes and all ready for their "overseas service."

The "nightclub set" made up the bulk of the guests, and another set, those who just didn't feel at home, comprised a second large portion. These were the ones who wanted rice for every meal. The smallest portion, which he called the "business set," paid no attention at all to matters outside official service. But they were all equally boring to him. Then there was that hassle of hanging around in clubs all night—the next day he always had a headache and felt sick to the stomach. But all this fell within his duties as a public servant, at least in the eyes of his guests, including Madam Murdono last night. Although she had been given instructions on how to arrange a meeting with the police force, which in her case meant the vice squad, she still wanted to compile her own "eyewitness" account. And he of course had to accompany her.

In one night Madam Murdono, who was going to eradicate prostitution, wanted to see as much as possible that related to her mission: the red-light district (a term she pronounced as if it were her own most original discovery) and a wide range of nightclubs— in short, she wanted to see everything in just one night. And our young attaché had no choice but to be her willing companion.

The attaché drew up a specific schedule. He chose a number of red-light districts, based on things he had heard, because some were classier than others. According to his plan, it all needed to be over by one in the morning. Then he could return home to his wife, who had long considered the work of entertaining guests from the homeland to be an insult to her husband because they always ended up in a nightclub. It wasn't that she was a jealous wife or that she was overly pious but that all these things weren't of interest to her, and that going to these places night after night was a bore, especially in the company of people who watched it all with the wide-eyed excitement of country bumpkins. But her husband would just say, "What can I do? It's part of the job."

And so he had set out with his guest last night, feeling as though he were showing someone around the zoo. He had ventured into places that he himself would never have gone, had it not been for the woman whose ambition it was to eradicate prostitution.

He had allocated just fifteen minutes to watching the first striptease show, and then they would be off to see another one. Of course he still bought tickets for the whole show, and they went in. They had arrived a little late, and it was standing room only. This felt like an insult, inflicted by himself upon himself. But the noble Madam Murdono was already up on her toes, thoroughly absorbed in the show. He was amazed at how long she could stand like that. Only once in a while did she lower her heels and stand normally. When one act was finished, it was only two or three seconds before the next one began, and soon fifteen minutes were up. He reminded her that it was time to move on. But she wanted to keep watching and said, "This is even more scandalous than London," and our junior diplomat was forced to give in. Which shot his schedule to pieces. So he had to skip a few of the other stops and proceed to the final event: *Les Naturistes*. According to what he had heard, this nightclub was among the most scandalous of them all. To quote his other guests: "They're stark naked, brother!"

The room was small and all the seats were taken, about thirty of them surrounding a small circular stage where the action was unfolding. There was a comedian cracking jokes alongside scandalous scenes in which the dancers alternately stripped and then teased the audience by covering up too much.

Madam Murdono kept commenting on the show. "That one has given birth, hasn't she?" And this was followed by a detailed anatomical description. Suddenly a young man standing with them at the bar asked, "U spreekt Hollands?"

Right there, in that very moment, it struck him once again—but this time with a feeling of shame—that it was as though his country and people still weren't free. Dutch colonialism had ended, but they were still dominated by foreign forces. It surprised him. He thought of himself as quite self-possessed and self-confident. But he was also now aware of the shame he felt. He had been reminded of it by his charge's Dutch-language chatter, all of it overheard by this Dutch kid. Certainly, as far as he could tell, this young blond Netherlander was no more than a kid. Furious, he told Madam Murdono he had a headache and it was time to go. She followed, annoyed.

They went out into the bustling street, into a night of neon signs and letters. The surfeit of nightclub advertisements—with lighted tubes shaped, for example, like a woman's bare leg—flickered on and off in neon animation that seemed to shoot up into the night sky, beckoning guests from far and near. In front of the nightclub were two boys and a man dressed like a priest ogling a picture of a nearly nude woman that had been placed in a lighted glass case.

For a second, he looked at the two boys (who might have been brothers living nearby) and the man in the priest's garb (who was gazing at pictures as if they were trees on his lawn) and compared them to his guest, the woman who had traveled halfway around the world to attend to these moral issues.

A street fair was underway next to the nightclub, and a few of the browsers were walking by, acting drunk and singing as they went. Madam Murdono said, "God have mercy! There's so much moral degeneracy here!"

Somehow, the junior diplomat felt that the insult was also aimed at him. He couldn't have explained why, had anyone asked him just then. He hailed a passing cab, but it was already taken.

"Would you like to go to the ballet or a concert tomorrow?" said our junior diplomat. He was a bit embarrassed at himself for putting on "cultural airs" like this. To be honest, he wasn't much interested in these "artistic" pursuits. He just liked watching soccer and things like that, even back in Jakarta.

"But isn't that what we just saw?" she asked. Our young diplomat was speechless. A man dressed as a nightclub doorman had walked over to them while thumbing through some pictures he was holding. He offered the pictures with the hand movements of a magician and said in English, "Nice photos."

At this, Madam Murdono began asking more questions.

The junior diplomat just wanted to leave.

"Should we buy them?" she urged.

"What for? They're porno pictures just like we saw inside."

"As documentation," she answered.

Her reply had the force of an order, so the junior diplomat felt he couldn't refuse. In the taxi back to Madam Murdono's hotel, our friend the diplomat remained silent. He was quiet for such a long time that eventually Madam Murdono took the lead, asking him in a voice that was both accusing and wheedling, "Why are you against the eradication of prostitution?"

"When did I say that?"

"Why, your whole attitude seems disapproving of my work!"

"Well . . . ," the junior diplomat replied, "I like prostitutes."

And although he knew that the driver didn't understand what they were saying, he couldn't help but imagine the man sporting a wide grin as he drove the car.

Translated by Brian Russell Roberts

6

SNOW IN PARIS

He threw the blanket back, feeling as if he hadn't slept at all. The dark room was filled with a white light. Outside, the city was covered with snow. Was it still falling? He sat up and searched with his feet for his slippers. The floor was as cold as ice. In the shop below he could hear Madame Bonnet, the widow who owned the hotel, calling out.

"Monique!" She was calling for the maid.

He turned to the window. The snow fell against the damp glass, obscuring his view like flickering scratches on an old film. It was very cold and very quiet.

Standing, he made his way to the washbasin against the wall. Without thinking, he turned on the hot tap. The water burned his hand and he angrily drew it back, then turned on the cold tap. The sound of the water splashing into the basin, hot and cold together, revived him and warmed his blood a little. It was a very cold winter. He went and took his bathrobe from the hook behind the door.

The fragrance of talcum powder rose from the folds of the robe, like some forgotten past. For a moment, a pain tore at his heart.

He dragged himself back to the basin. It was empty. He had forgotten to put in the plug. There were a few long strands of hair at the bottom of the basin.

He went back to bed.

When he checked the time again, it was eleven o'clock. Monique had probably knocked at his door some time ago. Of course. He could hear the sound of the vacuum cleaner in room 15, next to his.

Hoping that Monique would come in, he sat up again. Monique knew everything and would say nothing. Madame Bonnet knew too, but Madame Bonnet was different. She was a widow and understood everything on the basis of her own experience. Monique had not had these experiences. She understood things intuitively. Her eyes were soft, she smiled, and she did the work expected of her every day.

Early in the morning she looked after Madame Bonnet's three children (two boys and a girl) and dressed them to go to the nearby parish school. She opened the door for André, the bar attendant, a retired chauffeur. She dusted the furniture. Then she woke the boarders. The sound of her shoes at the same time in the morning was one of those important, unnoticed things, which, like the water flowing through the pipes, you only heard when it stopped.

Ah, Monique wouldn't come back today.

Surprisingly, this cheered him. He began to whistle. The noise of the vacuum cleaner in the next room stopped and then started again. Louder and more obvious. He forgot Monique and went downstairs.

"Bonjour monsieur André, bonjour Madame!"

Had he greeted them or not? André placed a cup of coffee, "ground coffee" as he always stressed, in front of him. He had learned that the Indonesian did not like coffee extract.

Various customers came in. Almost all of them were drivers from the large service station under the building next to the hotel.

They calmly entered one by one, bringing the cold wind with them. The half-opened door sprang shut again. Rubbing their frozen hands together, they stamped their boots on the threshold to get rid of the mud and dirty snow.

"Bonjour!"

Then they climbed onto the round bar stools.

André served them coffee and wine. Some always drank wine and ate the bread rolls they had brought with them. Already big men, their size was magnified by their thick, shabby jackets.

He saw them in relation to André and the bar, the way André made coffee and poured the drinks, confidently but obediently. Every day.

But were the other days really the same as today? The various wine bottles in rows, behind André's handsome face and his full head of hair.

Cinzano, Dubonnet, and others in various colors.

No one said very much. He was part of a silent morning ritual that began again each day. It was as quiet as a country restaurant.

"Will you have lunch here today, monsieur, or shall I wrap you a roll?"

He shook his head, almost like a spoiled child, and, standing up, walked to the door. The door swung noisily back and closed behind him. Outside, the air was as cold as ice and immediately enfolded him. He was briefly undecided.

Should he turn right or left, or go to the center of the city? The snow was still falling. He could feel it stabbing against his ears and hair.

He had met her a few days ago. It was later in the day than this but snowing in exactly the same way. Perhaps five days ago. Yes, five days ago. Today is Tuesday. On Thursday.

He had been on his way to police headquarters, at the prefecture, to renew his alien's residence permit. It was something he had to do at certain times. Now he only needed to report once a year. He had lived in Paris for fifteen years.

It was easier to be granted permission to live in France as an artist. *Peintre*, painter, he wrote and indeed he was a painter, although he had not painted anything for the past five years.

He wanted to write poetry too. It seemed to him that Paris and all it contained invited one to be a poet. Meaning to write, to express one's feelings in a real poem.

That had never happened. Well, it had. Once. Five days ago, on the night he met the girl, when they were sitting on the terrace of a restaurant beside the River Seine, facing the Notre Dame, with its towers soaring into the sky, white in the falling snow and the spotlights from the field in front of it.

"A prayer thrust high into the sky," he had said. She wrote the words into a red notebook she took from her handbag.

He regretted the words. He was embarrassed but didn't say anything.

Had they really met? Lived four nights together?

After leaving the prefecture, having renewed his visa, he had hesitated at a gateway opposite the Marché aux Fleurs, the flower market. Through the snow he saw a woman approaching him from the other side of the road. She stopped nervously in front of him and they briefly looked at each other.

He could not explain what was happening. But the look in the woman's eyes somehow added to his surprise and he turned unconsciously to buy a newspaper, the *Paris Presse*, from the vendor, a cripple who always ran the stand. Year after year he had lived in a dream. His mind whirled about like the snow, separating him from the bustle of the enormous city and locking him into a tiny space inhabited only by the figure of this woman. Everything outside that space was a figment of his imagination. He looked at the lead coin in his hand. Only that was real.

Was she speaking to him?

"Monsieur, do you speak English?"

He was briefly startled. How long had it been since anyone had spoken to him?

"Yes."

The girl—she was still young—explained her situation. She wanted to apply for a visa to go to Switzerland. Having come from London, she had decided to extend her journey once she had reached Paris. But she had no photographs and the officials needed a photograph. The requirement only applied to Asians. Europeans didn't need a visa. What race was she? Mixed?

"Suives moi!" he said reassuringly, waving his hand. Without realizing, he was speaking French. But the girl understood and was now walking beside him. He knew a photographer on an island in the middle of the Seine, near Notre Dame and several other important buildings. Ready "in ten minutes."

They walked toward the road beside the Notre Dame cathedral, turned left into a small street, entered a gate, and then crossed a narrow, dark yard. This was where the photographer worked, as indicated by the sign in English *HERE for your passport-photos* and the pointing figure of a hand.

Inside, the girl removed her overcoat. He could see that she was slender, attractive. Her sweater was wine red.

He stood in the corner of the studio, like a guide accustomed to serving tourists, watching her as she took out a comb, mirror, and her makeup.

A few minutes later the girl was standing ready to have her photograph taken. Now he could observe her from the side. Her face, her hair, breasts, hands, feet.

The impression was suddenly inconclusive. She was pretty but was she married? How old was she? She had both a child's simplicity and a woman's maturity and firmness.

The camera snapped twice and they only needed to wait. Their eyes met and he looked away.

"I would like to make a phone call. Can you help me, please? I can't use the Paris directory. It is not like the London book."

"What number?"

"I don't know. The Empire Hotel."

There were six Empire Hotels listed in the directory.

He asked the girl for the address of the hotel. She didn't know.

"What is it near? What important building, I mean?"

"Near the Saint Lazare station."

Finally they found it. Or at least found one worth trying.

"Who would you like to speak to, miss?" he asked, covering the mouthpiece with his hand.

"Mr. Stone, room 115."

He was startled but hid his surprise. And even more startled to hear the clerk say that Mr. Stone had paid for the room and checked out.

When he explained the situation to the young woman, she made no response. They paid for the photographs and left without saying anything else.

He felt as though they had known all about each other for a long time and were old acquaintances. Unconsciously, perhaps because of the cold, they walked close together.

On reaching the police station, he read the girl's name: Margareth Rodrigo.

"My name is Machmud."

The girl looked at him for a moment.

"Are you Indonesian?"

"Yes."

"I'm Filipina."

"I saw your passport."

Outside again, they wandered aimlessly through the falling snow.

"Do you still want to go to Switzerland?"

"No." He understood.

"Come and have a drink."

That was it. Five days ago. That night, he took her back to his hotel. They met Madame Bonnet on the stairs. He didn't introduce the girl. Madame Bonnet smiled and her smile seemed to bless them. She always smiled except when her children annoyed her.

"*Mignon*," Madame said to no one in particular. Cute. She continued down the stairs.

Margareth was indeed beautiful. She gave herself like a cat seeking warmth on a cold night.

Bonnet's "family" accepted the new situation. Just as they had accepted him without asking any questions. But this time he wanted them to ask him how and why. Monique addressed Margareth as "Madame."

It was all very friendly. Margareth accepted the way they treated her as her natural right.

During those few days, Margareth followed him everywhere he went in town, as he met his friends, borrowed money, and visited the embassy on the half day a week he worked there, making stenciled copies of information brochures to be sent to other embassies and official organizations, where they would probably never be read but simply thrown away, just as he tore up the brochures from other embassies as soon as they arrived.

Nobody asked him anything.

He wanted them to ask, just as he wanted to ask her questions.

He wanted Aimée, the Jewish girl, to ask how and why he had disappeared the past few days. Aimée was nice but she was as hard as iron. She wore long sleeves to cover the numbers the Germans had tattooed under her fine skin when she was imprisoned in

Buchenwald. He wanted them to ask him about love, faithfulness, betrayal, and friendship. But no one asked. He himself had long ago stopped asking about such matters.

He wanted to ask Margareth questions. But Margareth seemed to have no need to ask anything and was silent. She told him nothing about herself. He was living inside a story and he wanted to escape. He wanted to be set free. But Margareth said nothing. Neither of them said anything.

Tonight he was determined he would ask her about herself or tell her about himself.

Because the day was cold and Margareth was tired, he had gone to "work" alone. And he wanted to be alone just then.

On his way downstairs, he met Monique.

"Is Madame awake?"

"Leave her. Wake her at eleven. But please take her some coffee now . . . Er, and tell her that I'll be back at six."

But just before six that night, when he entered a restaurant near the metro station for a customary drink, he met Wong. He was annoyed.

He didn't like meeting Wong. Especially not now. Wong was Indonesian-Chinese but he could already see himself in this older man.

Wong had spent twenty years in Paris. He took his wife, a French woman, back to Indonesia after she had graduated from the Sorbonne—perhaps she hadn't graduated at all. She had left him, after living two years in Jakarta. And now Wong, like a character in a novel, was still searching for her among the six million inhabitants of Paris.

Twenty years. No one knew whether the story was true or not, whether he ever found her and, most surprising of all, what Wong did for a job and where he got his money.

Wong's life seemed to mirror Machmud's future, although Machmud couldn't explain precisely how. He had not married, not had a wife the way Wong had. But they shared something in common. He couldn't deny that. But he had never tried to understand the feeling. He just knew that he didn't like meeting Wong. Not just because Wong was completely bald, not because Wong wore glasses and had wrinkles around his mouth. And not because of the sad, patient, and sometimes mischievous look in his eyes. He often felt sorry for Wong, especially when Wong asked him to pay for his coffee, as he often did, especially in this restaurant.

But there was Wong, standing with his back to the entrance, in front of the cashier. Oh, he was placing a bet on a horse race.

He tried to leave at once but Wong turned and saw him across the cigarette smoke and the murmuring of voices. He was caught in Wong's gaze and sullenly entered the café.

For a long time, he was forced to listen to Wong telling him what he would do with the millions of francs he could win from betting on the horses and such like.

At ten he finally arrived home. There was no one downstairs. André had apparently gone out the back. He climbed the stairs quickly. His heart was beating rapidly. He knew. It was not simply an intuition.

The room was tidy, the air warm and moist. It was empty of all signs of humanity except for the traces of everyday boredom. Cleaned, slept in, cleaned, slept in. The room never spoke, never asked questions, and never answered any.

He went downstairs. André had returned and seemed extremely busy arranging the bottles on a shelf. Monique avoided his gaze. Madame Bonnet was nowhere to be seen. Everything stopped and revolved around his loneliness as he stared at the marble tables.

That was last night. He walked through the snow. Letting the buses pass him by.

The snow lay thick on the roads and the rooftops of Paris. He walked, then turned around and stared at his footprints. Two doves flew anxiously about, looking for food on the snow-covered ground.

The snow fell, gradually filling his footprints, covering the mud, turning everything white again. As white as the lonely path in front of him.

Translated by Harry Aveling

7

FONTENAY AUX ROSES

When I think about it now, my meeting her was not a coincidence but something I hoped would happen. Let me tell you about it. At the time I was renting a room on Rue B. The room was on the fourth floor and faced out to the world through a small window. The window pointed to the back wall of another building, across a dirty, square courtyard.

From my window, if I stood and looked slightly upward, I could see another window. That window was dirty too. It had no curtain and was almost always closed. But there was a small pot on the sill filled with flowers. At least there was in summer, which it now was.

All of the windows on the wall opposite were like boxes and had thin, dirty, gray curtains. One was adorned with flowers. That wasn't the only thing that drew my attention to the window. I was surprised that the window was seldom open even though it was summer, and when it was open, even though only a little, I never saw who opened it. The pane behind the flowerpot always remained closed. But beyond that, there was another even more important reason why I looked toward the slightly opened window on hot summer afternoons. For as long as I had been in my room, six months, almost every afternoon, toward six o'clock, I always heard someone playing the piano. They played well but still practiced in order to play even better. Having grown accustomed to the music, I didn't give it much thought, although the sound of the piano, which I assumed came from the building opposite, had soothed my feelings from the very beginning. And from the very beginning, I connected it with the flowerpot, for some reason.

I started renting my room in winter. And only when summer was well advanced, six months later, did I realize that my room faced west because I could see the rays of the sun shining at an angle onto the pot in the morning as I hung my bathrobe and blanket out to air. In winter, one seldom saw the rays of the sun, or the sun itself. The part of the city in which I lived was normally very quiet as well.

It was like living in a village, an isolated place in a city of millions where the not-too-poor and the not-too-rich lived far from the bustle of the large boulevards. Nor was it as grimy as the suburbs of the industrial zones, which had their own particular sounds.

The village peacefulness had been attractive, as was the cheap rent. I liked the calm and the sense of simplicity. I should say that I knew very well what it was like to live in a real village, the boredom of it all, and I didn't think I could do it anymore. I enjoyed the crowds and activity of a city of millions of people, the sense of not knowing everyone else or being known by them. That seemed to me to be true freedom. And at that time, I really enjoyed that sort of freedom.

But there were also times when the rural-like atmosphere was very oppressive, just like living in a real village, without the cackling of hens after laying an egg, the barking of dogs, and without the rustle of the wind through the leaves. Only the emptiness of a city of millions of people on a hot afternoon. The silence and the hard faces turned to stone.

Now, after living in a true village away from the city, I can see that my enjoyment of the noise and the crowds in the city was due to my reluctance to be involved with anyone or anything, and perhaps my unwillingness to shoulder any responsibility. I wanted to be free.

But that afternoon, that summer afternoon, I needed a friend, someone to talk to, go places with, when everyone else was on holiday, visiting the public gardens or the forests or the countryside. But my circumstances didn't allow me to do any of those things, and so I gazed hopefully at the window across the courtyard. Hopefully because the flowerpot was still there; had its owner gone away for a long holiday out of town, the pot would have been taken in and given to a neighbor to look after.

It was almost six o'clock and I suddenly realized that I couldn't hear the piano, and hadn't heard it for several days. That made me feel even more lonely. And I decided to go out, to share in some of the excitement of the city. Suddenly the window opposite opened and I saw . . . Angelique. I found out her name later. She was small and slim, attractive but not pretty, and had long, black hair.

Her face was pale, unwell, and she was not wearing any makeup. Her eyes lit up briefly when she saw me; then she vanished back into her room and reappeared carrying a cup. She watered the flowers. When she had finished, she looked at me. For a moment, I was uncertain. Then I gestured with my hands, like a person playing the piano and, after a short while, she looked at me again, nodded, and closed the window. My heart beat faster than it had ever done before and I too closed my window, withdrew into silence, lost in thought, hoping I would hear her playing the piano. But the silence continued and I remembered that her body had been covered with a sheet. She must have been sick to wrap herself up like that on such a hot day, I thought, and then I went out to catch some of the bustle of the city.

The next afternoon, I met her.

After I had described what she looked like, and her floor level, about the fifth floor, the concierge told me the girl's name and room number, adding "the existentialist!" in a proud but gossipy way. But perhaps he was describing me too, because my appearance was exactly the same as those called "existentialists."

My thick short hair, carefully trimmed beard, dark t-shirt which was intended to hide the dirt, my uncertain origin, and my lack of an occupation, apart from drinking coffee and talking all day, because coffee was cheaper than anything else but water, and refreshing enough. Existentialists: the young bore the name of the fashionable "philosophy" in a city where philosophers had flourished and fought throughout the ages, Paris. Like the other young existentialists, I never thought about existentialism. I simply felt that we agreed with the philosophy's founder, a man called Sartre, that life, including the world, nature, and humanity, was absurd, and that no good reason could be found to justify it, even if you could be bothered to look for one. I don't know if that was what existentialism was really about. That was how we explained it. In general, we were pseudo-intellectuals, read a lot, and in Paris, on the basis of a moderate education, and moderate intelligence, could dive into all the philosophies there had ever been or ever would be, and all the works of literature as well, so we believed, so I believed. The whole of life could be spent reading, and at that time this was all I did and all that I thought was worth doing. The rest of our time was for fun. If we wanted to live, we lived through our bodies, feeling our muscles, blood and bones, the lungs that helped us to talk. We danced, debated, fought, made love. What else was there to do? If we had money, we became spectators, spectators of life, life played out on the stage: the theater, opera, or silver screen. It was easier than reading. We worked to earn money, but only enough to meet our needs. A small amount of time was enough to fill our bellies. We followed one basic principle: do as little physical labor as possible in order to have as much time as possible to pursue cultural activities, create art, write literature, think—think about the human condition, think about the secrets we each contained, think, think. As an illustration of the meaning for which we were searching, we had the theater. Watching life on the stage called for a change in the way we lived. But it was too late to have our own adventures—go to war, win a colony, conquer some uncivilized race. Instead, we would have had to fight against people in Indo-China who wanted to be free, just as we did. It was no longer possible to explore new continents. Scientific discoveries belonged to the experts. There were not many Mount Everests. There were no more unknown lands to be mapped, or poles and oceans. Almost all the plants and animals on the land, sea, and air had been classified. Those sorts of tasks were increasingly the work of a few specialists. All that was left for us to explore were the worlds of thought and philosophy, as free individuals with the same rights as the original thinkers and philosophers, the freedom of our own rooms and the darkened theater, where everyone was equal in the debates with those thinkers, philosophers, and poets. If our opportunities were so narrow that we did nothing at all, that was not our fault.

Doing nothing: that was how I felt. Doing nothing meant more than being unemployed. It was a culture in which no one worked, and, as everyone knows, culture involves every aspect of one's life. From cutting one's fingernails to thinking about the world to come, and diving deep into the human soul.

But the words "doing nothing" only became meaningful once I started living in this village, outside Paris.

As I climbed the steps to Angelique's room, because the lift was broken, I felt disappointed. At that time, I didn't very much like existentialist youths. I didn't believe that they had really considered their position as unemployed. And I especially didn't care for those who criticized them but gawked anyway, the American tourists, and pious folks from the countryside who came to Paris to visit prostitutes then returned home, cursing Paris again.

But I kept climbing. I needed Angelique as someone I could talk to, or ask not to talk.

When she opened the door and invited me in, she smiled, the smile of an older woman, receiving a child who had fallen in love with her. "Poseur!" I thought.

After introducing ourselves, and discussing my room and work, she had no option but to play the piano. Briefly. Then she coughed. Tuberculosis, I concluded when I looked at her pale face in the lamplight.

"I haven't long to live!" she said, lighting a cigarette (no wonder, I thought), without offering one to me. Her every action fit the general image of an independent Parisian woman. And she knew it. She seemed to be acting a part in a play, knowing that she had an audience. I invited her to come out with me, to go to a café for coffee.

"I would cough all the time!" she said but finally decided to go and we went.

She told me the story of her life, of course. The child of a small shopkeeper, with big ambitions to become a solo pianist. From Milan. She was Italian. I didn't ask her anything else. We sat thinking, doing nothing.

After that we often went out together. And I learned that she was like many other young men and women: she was clever and well informed, perhaps too well informed!—it was more than her sweet small body could bear. Her spirit was vast but her body had not grown because she had not had enough vitamins or sunlight or fresh air, and the inevitable consequence had been tuberculosis.

"Why don't you go home?" I asked her. "Back to the hills and sunlight of Italy?"

"Sometimes you can't go home again," she said very dramatically, and I realized that I wanted to know more, to dig more deeply.

But no matter how skillfully I probed, I only learned more about what she thought and not about what she had experienced. Perhaps she had not experienced anything important, I later decided. People who live in constant illusions become psychological cripples.

To have experiences means to become a person. The person is the individual who meets other people, who meets life. Not to meet other people, meet life, through love, responsibility, and anger, meant that one had never begun to be an individual. Was Angelique an individual?

I thought about these different things each time we met.

Finally she told me, showing neither sincerity nor mockery, that Angelique was not her real name. She called herself that because she was close to death, on her way to heaven. I had no desire to ask her real name.

I once asked her whether she believed in heaven, simply for the sake of asking. "Yes," she replied. "But there is no hell," she added with a sigh, as if this disappointed her. She believed in God and gave a simple reason: Why is an apple shaped like an apple?

Then she was silent for a while and looked sideways at me. And she said, "It doesn't exist. Heaven doesn't exist. There is nowhere to return to. There is no paradise lost."

The condition of her health and the approach of autumn, season of decay, made her think more often of the afterlife. The yellow leaves would soon harden and fall, and once winter came the rain on the asphalt would soon become ice. I smiled, spontaneously. Why is an apple shaped like an apple? Why is Angelique? I thought playfully.

Very early one morning, after we had spent the night dancing and drinking at a dance hall, she took me to a nearby church. And she truly prayed. As though she wanted me to watch her praying, she left me at the entrance and went to kneel in the middle of the church. Then we left.

The trees were completely bare, and we walked close together along the edge of the river as the cold wind blew. She coughed. "Heaven means not knowing," she said. "Hell is praying in a church the way I did.

"We know that we will never know until we die. Or when we are very old, and our body and blood need nothing more. When you are very old, you should live in the countryside."

I made no comment. In fact, I was a little annoyed. I wanted to sleep.

"But everything has an end, its own form of death, in God. If you don't die young, I hope you can live in a quiet village, with trees and the light."

Had I been more used to such chatter, I wouldn't have noticed, but, in fact, her words suddenly made me aware of the pleasure of the clear blue early morning sky. A vast blue, more vast than the happiness and hope in my heart.

My smile faded when she coughed. She said, "But if you reach heaven, don't forget what you once had, don't forget them. Heaven is only perfect when one remembers the precious things one has lost."

A few days later, I was startled when I went to see Angelique and the concierge told me that she had died. She hadn't committed suicide, as I first suspected. She had coughed up a lot of blood. And her body had already been taken away, he didn't know where. The concierge closed the door. Angelique was dead.

A few days later again, I received a letter from Fontenay aux Roses, a rather pleasant name for a village. Close to Paris. Surrounded by hills. Quiet. The sort of place where I thought I would like to spend my old age. I had visited there in winter, while the snow was falling and the village was covered in white. I was briefly reminded of my visit as I opened the letter.

The letter offered me the use of a room. It was a friendly letter. "The room is not a large room but I think it should be large enough for your needs." A short letter. Who wrote it? The signature was not clear. A woman.

I decided to go, and not just because of Angelique's passing. I could try it for a few months, I thought, remembering Angelique's words. I was slightly sad.

Before finally leaving, I glanced at the window on the other side of the courtyard. The flowerpot had gone. A pure white curtain covered the window. I went. The seasons were changing and Fontenay aux Roses felt particularly beautiful. Of course it was simply an ordinary village. An ordinary village with which I had no connection, where I felt like a stranger. If I had seen it from a quickly passing train, it would have looked rather boring. Perhaps it would have given the impression of being inhabited by an important person who liked solitude, the sort of person one often reads about in books, or just a very ordinary village where one occasionally heard the creaking of a passing bullock cart, the cackle of hens, and the barking of a dog, and at certain times of day, the roar of a train behind the hills, coming and going, but invisible.

That was certainly my impression as I entered the village, carrying my suitcase. An impression that intensified as I approached the house indicated in the letter. A freestanding, two-story house on the slope of a hill facing toward Paris in the distance. The house and yard were uncared for and rather deserted. Apart from the woman who opened the door, there was no sign of anyone else. If one wanted to live in solitude, I thought to myself, this was the ideal place, and I turned and looked back toward Paris.

I was startled by the first words the woman spoke as she warmly took my suitcase. I still remember how my blood raced when I heard her say: "I am Angelique's mother. Welcome. So you are the friend she has told me so much about."

Angelique's mother? Was she Italian?

As we ate, Angelique's mother talked. She told stories the way Angelique did. I learned a lot about their family, a French family, original inhabitants of Fontenay aux Roses.

Angelique's father died as a partisan, resisting the German Nazis. Her brother, her only brother, had been in jail for ten years, having been a German spy, and would stay there for the rest of his life.

"Perhaps Angelique told you that she wanted to be a doctor, a chest specialist," the old woman said. "But she was always sick and never received the scholarship she wanted. So she studied the piano. Anyway, it would have been too hard to be a doctor."

"She played the piano well," I said, perhaps to console her. "She had talent."

Then the old woman said: "Of course you'd like to see her grave."

"To . . . morrow," I said, "when it is lighter." I was still thinking that Angelique had always appeared to be so honest when she was talking. Had she said she came from Mexico, I would have believed her.

No matter what, I felt that she believed what she said about death and heaven.

The next day the old woman apparently forgot that she had invited me to visit Angelique's grave. I was glad she had forgotten. Because I never wanted to see the grave. And I never have visited the grave, even though it is in the yard near the house, according to her mother. When the mother asked whether I had visited the spot, I simply said, "Yes."

Several months passed. I still had not visited the grave.

Then, in spring, as the flowers blossomed, I noticed the grave from my window, as I stared toward Paris in the distance.

And as if she were standing next to me, I heard Angelique whisper, "Heaven is remembering what you once had."

I have now lived in Fontenay aux Roses for three years.

Translated by Harry Aveling

8

THE INTERNATIONAL TRAIN

The train had just crossed from France into Belgium. "Please, play again," said the middle-aged woman opposite to the young man next to me. He didn't understand English, and as though in search of an explanation he leaned his arms on his guitar and looked across at his companion, a sailor like himself.

His friend, the older of the two, said something to him in a language I didn't understand, and he took up his guitar again.

The girl on my left was looking out the window, lost in her own thoughts. Opposite her sat another girl, to the right of the woman who'd asked the young sailor to keep on playing.

I watched her as she followed the movements of his fingers over his guitar strings. The older sailor was studying my face.

"Indian?" he asked, while his friend played on.

"No, Indonesian," I said, turning in his direction.

"I'm Greek, like my friend here," he said, pointing to the guitar player. The music stopped.

"Oh, you gentlemen are Greek?" said the middle-aged woman. Her words caught the attention of the girl on my left and the other girl sitting opposite her. We all focused on the sailors: Greeks!

It was as though all of us had spoken the word in surprise.

"We have Greeks here! This gentleman is Indonesian, and I'm Flemish," the woman said. "And this young lady, I presume, is Dutch."

"Yes, I am," said the girl next to me.

"Now it's your turn," said the woman to the girl on her right. "What nationality are you?"

Shifting in her seat, the girl replied, "I'm German." Then she turned and fixed her eyes on me.

"Where are you from? I didn't catch what you said just now."

"I'm Indonesian," I said, as the thought "What an attractive girl!" flashed through my mind.

"Who would have thought," said the older of the two sailors, turning our attention back to the German girl. "You look Latin!"

We all took stock of the girl's beauty. She was tall but well proportioned. Her eyes were like those of a deer living untrammeled in the forest.

"Thank you," she said evenly, turning her gaze to the spring countryside we were passing through.

It was a beautiful day, and it felt as if the moment, and even the day itself, had been created especially for her. The strains of the young man's guitar began to blend with the youthful glow of this Rhine maiden.

"Different nations have different ideas about beauty," said the Dutch girl next to me. "Even so, I wouldn't have thought that you two here were Greeks! I always imagine Greeks to be . . ."

"We're only sailors, miss," said the Greek.

"What—in your opinion—makes someone attractive?" the Flemish woman asked the Dutch girl. She didn't seem to be looking for an argument. It was clearly all in fun.

"Who knows? I'm just thinking of the pictures of Greek heroes when I was at school," said the Dutch girl.

"Heroes are always handsome," the woman replied. "But you couldn't say that Socrates was handsome. Take this gentleman from Indonesia as an example. In your opinion, is he a Socrates or a hero?"

"That's hard to say," the girl said, looking at me in profile with a twinkle in her eye. "But side on, I'd say this gentleman was handsome, even though he looks like an artist from Montmartre. Might you be a painter?

"Or an actor?" she added quickly.

"Neither," I said, causing each of my traveling companions to smile in my direction. "A student?" the woman suggested as I looked at each of the others in turn, saving the German girl for last. I was wondering how I would place each of the three women. Judging by her simple clothes and her assertiveness, I took the Dutch girl next to me to be a young woman on her way home from a working holiday in Paris, where she'd had a job as a waitress. I imagined her expecting to have some adventures while she was away but never actually going ahead with anything, because in her heart she wasn't really ready. The German girl, I was sure, was the daughter of wealthy parents. She was well dressed in expensive clothes, and her pampered skin suggested a life that wanted for nothing. Her facial features, as well as her refined speech, bespoke the intelligence that comes from a good education. The Flemish woman was the wife of someone quite well-to-do, maybe a middle manager in a firm somewhere; in any case, a married woman. But why was she traveling alone?

Meanwhile, they were all awaiting my reply. "I'm a traveler," I said. This seemed to leave them somewhat confused.

"So in that case, you're a very wealthy man," the Dutch girl said. The conversation was entirely in English, which everyone accepted as a matter of course as our language of communication. "You've got stickers on your case from hotels in Tokyo, Los Angeles, New York and . . . what's that? 'The Hawaiian Hotel'?"

The German girl had already turned her attention to other things, and the others no longer seemed very interested in knowing the truth, so I just said, "No, I'm not rich—friends put me up everywhere I go." That seemed to be enough for the Dutch girl and the others, but the German girl suddenly focused in on the conversation. She looked straight at me and asked, "Have you been in America?"

"I left New York two weeks ago," I said. "So you were only briefly in Paris?" she continued. "Did you like it there?"

"How about you? Do you like Paris?" I asked in return, and I could see the others prick up their ears in anticipation of her reply.

"I . . . didn't really like it," she said quietly.

"Is this the first time you've been?" I asked.

"Yes," she said without elaborating.

"Were you on your own?" asked the Dutch girl.

"Oh, I've got a friend there," came the reply.

"I was disappointed with Paris too," the Dutch girl went on. "People go on and on about how beautiful it is, but huh! It's so dirty, and the men . . . you've really got to watch yourself! French people are really stupid, especially the rich ones."

"It sounds like you had a summer job with a French family," the Flemish woman suggested.

"Yes, I did. It was pure slavery! Spoiled, whiny kids and a master and mistress with nothing to do all day and night except lie around pressing the bell for every little whim that came into their heads. Eating whatever they pleased, and going off into the country for breaks at their chateau. No wonder France is bankrupt! All they're good at is barking orders at servants." And laughing out loud, she went on, "Can you imagine, whenever we went driving in the country we had to take along a potty. And when the kids used it to do their business, we'd have to stop at a restaurant to take it to the toilet. The master and his wife would go on and on, arguing over anything and everything. French people are completely useless. Compare that with what you find in Holland. It's only now I really understand: in Holland the fields are more beautiful and the cows are fatter than the best that France has to offer. As far as I can see, France is done for."

"Don't let your feelings run away with you, miss," I said. "What do you think, madam?" The two Greek sailors were playing the part of observers.

"Oh, sir. Paris is a city for young people," the Flemish woman replied. "Everyone should experience it while they're young."

"Experience it?" said the Dutch girl angrily. "What is there to experience there except men who expect the full service from you, the first time you meet them? Want you to meet up with them somewhere in the metro? Yech! Especially that Algerian student. A real sleaze!"

She paused a moment, and then added, "I hope he dies waiting."

"So you did say you'd meet him? You shouldn't make promises you don't intend to keep," I teased her.

"Well, if you turn them down they won't let you go. If you want to get away, you have to agree to a date," she said.

"Do you really think he's still there waiting for you?" asked the Flemish woman.

The Dutch girl didn't answer. Then, with a note of hesitation in her voice, she said, "Anyway, there's no guarantee he *was* a student!"

"Can you tell the difference between an Algerian and a Negro?" asked the Greek sailor, chiming in on the conversation. All of us except the German girl—who kept her eyes on the scenery outside—turned to look at him.

"To me they're all the same," said the Dutch girl. "Take this gentleman here for example. You can't tell whether he's Chinese, Indian, or Negro."

"That's true, miss," I said. "You're right. Just imagine, I was once taken for . . . a Greek. What do you think of that?"

They all smiled, unsure whether I was joking. Then they burst out laughing, all except for the German girl, who didn't react at all.

"It's true," said the woman opposite. "If you look at him front on, you wouldn't know what nationality this Indonesian gentleman is, other than something that goes with his brown skin. I suppose he's a kind of . . . Othello."

"Othello? The Negro in that opera?" said the Dutch girl. "Oh yes, you're right. He's an Othello!" She brightened up at the idea.

"Yes, Othello from Shakespeare's tragedy," the Flemish woman said. "Meanwhile, your own Othello is waiting around somewhere in the metro, singing an aria of revenge." At this, the compartment filled with noisy laughter. The German girl looked uneasy. Then everything went quiet, as though no one knew what to say. The young Greek started improvising on his guitar. He wasn't able to follow all the conversation, and he looked a bit confused. His friend got up and stepped out into the corridor to stretch. The German girl opened a white handbag and took out a mirror. She examined herself and did a quick touch-up, as though she were about to step outside too, but then sat back as she was. The Dutch girl took out a sandwich and began to eat.

"Would you like some?" she asked me.

"No thanks," I replied. "I'm not hungry."

The Flemish woman took out a chocolate bar and began to eat too. The German girl drew a deep breath, but without making it obvious. For some time the compartment was completely quiet.

Then, between bites of chocolate, the Flemish woman asked me, "This isn't the first time you've been to Paris, is it?"

"No," I replied. "I spent a year there as a student five years ago."

"Did you like it?"

"Well, you know what it's like when you're young. Now it's all just a memory."

She smiled and looked at the German girl. "This gentleman knows his way around. It would have been nice if he could have kept you company while you were in Paris."

The German girl smiled, and then: "I don't doubt he could have shown me some interesting aspects of life in Paris. But I'm afraid that even then, I wouldn't have liked it. I don't know. I think it's got to do with the kind of person you are. I'm not the romantic type."

"I think you live too sheltered a life," I said. "I can see you in a big house and garden on the banks of the Rhine, not wanting for anything. I imagine you can go traveling whenever you like, seeing one country after another."

"Whatever you say, sir," she said.

"Ah, it's such a bother, traveling," said the Flemish woman. "In the end, it all gets a bit tedious. Wherever you go you know what places will be like, even before you've seen them. This isn't the age of Marco Polo. Everything's lost its romance these days. Just stay at home, I say. There's no need to go to faraway places."

"Have you been on vacation?" I asked.

"Yes," she said. "My husband and I drove down to the Riviera. But something came up at home, in Brussels. A telegram arrived, and I had to come back. My husband is following in the car."

All this talk about traveling suddenly put me in mind of the girl I knew in Paris who worked as a maid and year by year had managed to visit nearly every country in Europe. Wherever she went, she carried beautiful posters that she'd stolen from public places in Paris under the cover of darkness, to sell to collectors who paid high prices for them. When I first met her five years ago, she'd only been as far as England, but when I saw her again just recently she was still living in the same little room in an old hotel but had traveled all over Europe—apart from Italy—on the proceeds of her stolen posters.

"I'm going to Italy on my way to North Africa," she told me. "I'll end up in Ethiopia." She showed me a biography of Emperor Haile Selassie. "I just need a few more posters to make up the foreign currency reserves I'll be smuggling into Italy with me. *Ginet, La Voleuse*—'Ginet, the Thief'—that's the aristocratic name I'm going to write in the visitors' book in Haile Selassie's palace. I've got a letter of introduction from his nephew, who's studying here at the Sorbonne," she said.

"So you don't like Paris anymore?" The Flemish woman was talking to me again.

"No, not anymore," I said. "People grow up, don't they? If nothing else, advancing age makes you a realist. Duty calls," I laughed.

"Brussels, Brussels!" called the conductor.

She stood up, somewhat startled. "Dear me! I've been too absorbed in our conversation! Good-bye all . . ." She hurried away as the train pulled into the station. The young man with the guitar had gone off somewhere, but I knew he and his friend were on their way to Amsterdam to join the ship they were working on. The Dutch girl stood up too, saying, "I'm going to get some coffee."

That left only me and the German girl.

"Where are you getting off?" she asked me.

"What about you?" I returned the question.

"Maybe Antwerp, maybe Amsterdam," she said. "Anywhere at all, actually."

"Why's that?" I wondered. But out loud I said, "In that case, I'll get off wherever you do."

"Amsterdam then," she said. On the platform outside, I saw our Flemish friend embracing an older woman, probably her mother. The window of the compartment was slightly open, and through the gap I heard the older woman say, "So you've had another fight with that husband of yours?" before they both disappeared into the crowd.

With a paper cup of coffee in one hand, the Dutch girl stepped back inside the compartment, followed by the two Greeks. When I moved to make room for them I dislodged the guitar that had been leaning against me, and the German girl had to save it from falling on the floor.

"Thank you," I said. She gave the guitar to the young Greek, then sat down again. The train had started to move.

For a while no one said anything. I found myself thinking about the German girl's rather odd behavior.

A change of destination—a change of mind—was nothing to her. Antwerp or Amsterdam, no problem.

"Are you hungry? Would you like to go and get something to eat?" She broke the silence.

"Yes, that would be good. I need some fresh air," I said. She stood up and I followed her.

There were plenty of empty tables in the restaurant car. We chose a corner table and sat opposite one another. As she studied the menu, she remarked, "I think I'll get off in Antwerp after all. There's no point in me going on to Amsterdam. Antwerp is convenient. My brother lives there as a representative of my father's company. He—my father—lives in Hamburg, and I have a grandmother in Dusseldorf.

"Does that surprise you?" She looked at me as she asked the question, and it was only then that I realized she wasn't as young as I'd first thought. "To me a scattered family seems quite ordinary."

Just then the waiter appeared, serving us our soup and asking, "Would you like your steak well done or rare?"

"I'll have mine rare. What about you?" she asked. "The same," I replied.

She took a mouthful of soup, then stopped.

"Don't you like soup?" she asked. "This isn't very tasty, to be sure."

"Don't worry about it. I'd rather use the time to talk."

"So, you're a foreigner here. I know your country, even though I've never been there. I almost went, three years ago. My former fiancé—former, note—is living there at the moment. A place called Magetan. I don't know where it is exactly, but it's somewhere in the middle of Java."

"That's a long way from where I live. I'm in Jakarta. I've never been there."

"It sounds like a beautiful place. And not too hot."

"Yes, I'm sure it is."

"But it's too late now. Too bad. It's my own fault. I promised I'd follow him . . . to get married, six months after he left . . . but I never went. In the end, I wasn't brave enough to go against my father's wishes."

"Why wouldn't he agree?"

"Lots of reasons. Lots. Take a look at me. Look carefully. What do you see?"

I studied her face. And oh, what a pretty face it was!

"Don't you notice anything?" she asked with a smile. "Very well. My mother is Indonesian. She lives in Madiun . . . Yes, pure Indonesian. Do you understand? It was me who pushed my fiancé to take the job in Indonesia. My father wanted to cover up the fact that my mother is an Indonesian woman he left just before the Second World War broke out there. He brought me with him to Europe, and here I am. A Northern European, the daughter of a Nazi, a faithful follower of Hitler. If I could change, be you for example . . ."

"But aren't you of legal age? Can't you go wherever you want . . . ?" I asked.

"That's it. It all comes down to me. I was raised as a proper German girl. My looks help conceal my mixed origins. I've been given a good life. I can have anything I want, and I've never seen Indonesia, never even met an Indonesian person before . . . I was taken to Germany as a baby. You're the first Indonesian I've ever seen."

After that she fell silent and stayed that way for the remainder of the meal. When we returned to our seats she didn't sit down again. She picked up her bag and coat as the train approached Antwerp. Then she was gone, with just an "Auf Wiedersehen!" directed at everyone in the compartment.

A moment later the train was pulling into the station. The Dutch girl remarked, "I'm surprised that German girl turned out to be so friendly. She had that superior air . . . toward . . . forgive me sir, you especially."

"It's all right, I've been in Germany too," I said. "They aren't all like you imagine."

"Yes, I was thinking of the upper-class Germans. The Nazis," she said.

"Oh, I've never met upper-class people there."

"And anyway, it's not important. People everywhere have their golden ages at different times. Maybe in the centuries to come it will be the colored people's day. Maybe then you'll have to look like a Negro to be thought beautiful."

"Maybe," I said. "That may be the case, and it's a pity you didn't follow through with your promise to your own Negro."

Suddenly the old sailor broke his silence. "That German girl was really pretty. Beautiful!"

"Yes indeed," I said. "Like a Greek goddess."

"Ha ha ha," he burst out laughing. "You've been deceived, sir. Greek women are overweight and quite dark skinned. Do you know that Alexander the Great's armies brought back beautiful female slaves of all different hues from Asia? Ha ha ha . . . Apollo is only a myth. But that German girl was no myth. One in a million!"

The young man beside me packed his guitar away in a canvas bag and settled down to sleep. I moved to the empty seat opposite, where the German girl had been sitting. I felt sleepy. The others too prepared to sleep. The old sailor made himself comfortable in his corner of the compartment. The Dutch girl opened a book and took out her glasses.

I was asleep in a flash, carried off into dreams amid what remained of the German girl's perfume. I lost my sense of time . . . Suddenly I heard a surprise announcement: "Madiun! Madiun!" I looked out the window in a daze, expecting to see young boys selling snacks. I felt hot. Then everything changed, and I could see only the cool colors of spring. But in the hazy reflection in the glass there was still the image of a railway station in Indonesia, where a wizened old woman carried a big bamboo basket strapped to her body with a length of cloth. Then, another Indonesian station announcement: "Kroya! Kroya!" . . .

I was shaken awake. I stood up to open the window some more. It was too hot inside the compartment, and it was full of the old sailor's cigarette smoke, as he sat there watching his sleeping friend. The Dutch girl was nowhere to be seen.

The cool air rushed in, scouring me clean in heart and mind.

Translated by Keith Foulcher

9

COMBAT

This story takes place in 1947, two years after the outbreak of the Indonesian revolution and more than a year after power was wrested from the hands of Japanese colonialism. To the best of their ability at the time, the Indonesian people had put together a government administration and were organizing social life under the threat of Dutch attack. The attacks came from the cities the Dutch had occupied along the coasts, and were part of their attempts to recolonize Indonesia and its people. Under these conditions Indonesia faced a thousand and one different obstacles. Everything was done in an improvised manner and with a minimum of expertise. An elderly doctor found himself appointed district head; an enthusiastic village schoolteacher was instructed to form an army unit from a group of young men who'd never held a weapon in their lives. But the fire of revolution blazed on, and swept up everything in its path.

Nevertheless, amid that fervor there were sometimes quiet corners that never experienced the revolution directly in the form of armed combat with the Dutch, like the mountainous upland regions of Sumatra where this story takes place. The people of these regions all collected contributions in support of the revolution in the combat zones around the coastal cities, and the young men left in droves to enlist as soldiers for the cause. Most of them couldn't be absorbed into the ranks of the regular army, but they found places for themselves in the militia bands that sprang up alongside it. To aid their operations, these militias took responsibility for providing for themselves, supplementing the meager levels of support they received from the government, and picking up contributions from the people of the interior. Not all of them were fortunate enough to find sources of income like foreign-owned factories and plantations that had been abandoned and later requisitioned by the army and whose products became part of the smuggling trade across the Straits of Malacca to Singapore.

It is these militia bands that our story concerns. It begins in a small town in a mountain valley, when the militiamen were withdrawing to mount a guerrilla campaign in the face of enemy attacks in violation of the agreement that had been negotiated with the Indonesian side. This was the enemy's response to Indonesian demands for total independence. After their first general offensive, the previously peaceful situation in this mountain valley quickly changed. Now it felt as though they were living in a war zone, even though all they had seen to this point had been enemy planes. The troops retreating from the coast brought with them the climate of war, but it was the militia bands that were the main source of the changed atmosphere. They lacked any organization, and there were often disputes between them that resulted in small-scale combat. As they retreated, they would strip each other of weapons or fight over strategic locations for guerrilla activity—the hills close to the main roads and the valleys where people lived. It is important to remember that at this time Sumatra still had vast upland plains and forests that were devoid of human habitation.

The valleys were of interest to the militiamen because apart from being the areas where the towns were located, they were crossed by all the major roads. This meant that the different bands fought for control of these regions. It is one of those struggles that is the subject of the first part of the following story. It happened during the dry season, after the harvest and when the rice fields lay empty.

I

The possibility of armed conflict weighed heavily on the town and the minds of its inhabitants. For some days now people had been worried that fighting would break out between the local militia units that were dug in outside the town. After the enemy troops began to move away from the coast and push forward into the interior, the militias had appeared in bands numbering up to several hundred men, a big increase over the groups of twenty or thirty that had been turning up previously. They came on foot, across the mountains and through the forests. In the past, they'd only ventured into the interior in search of support from the local inhabitants in the form of money, clothing, and food supplies. Now they were pulling back to organize guerrilla action in the face of enemy attacks. All the main roads were controlled by enemy aircraft.

The fear that the enemy would broaden its line of attack was now becoming mixed up with fear of these local militiamen. They had a menacing look about them and there was no discipline in the way they were organized. They were entrenched close in around the town, taking over schools and houses belonging to the local people to meet their needs. It was even said that some of them had asked for churches to be turned into temporary barracks. The regional administration and the local army command were powerless to control them. The institutions of government and a functional regular army were still being established, and without any coordinated response to the latest enemy attacks there had been an influx of refugees from other areas. The refugees brought more chilling stories about what the militias had been up to, adding to what the townsfolk had themselves experienced in recent times. They were already familiar with the militiamen's fondness for playing around with weapons and their use of threats to elicit supplies and other forms of support.

It was only recently that a militia lieutenant colonel, a former policeman, had shot himself dead playing with his own pistol. The bullet went right through his mouth and came out the top of his head. It was also said that they sometimes settled disputes not with a duel but a surprise attack; there was one brigade commander who was shot from the underbrush while he was bathing in the river. The names they gave their brigades were themselves enough to make your hair stand on end: Flying Dragon, Lightning Bolt, Wild Tiger!

And now those tigers were roaming around quite close to the town. To make things worse, it seemed there was a dispute going on between two big units over who would make the town's school buildings their barracks—with all the comforts and advantages that would bring—and who would have to stay out in the villages. People said there were thousands of militiamen out there encircling the town.

None of the commanders would have been able to give a precise figure for the number of troops in his unit. At best he might be able to give an approximation. People estimated that with the inclusion of the family members they'd brought with them, the total number of people in the militia bands was in the order of three thousand. These three thousand were under two different commands, known as Lightning Bolt and White Buffalo. Previously, before the enemy's first general offensive, they were under the command of a single major general acting outside the regular army.

But then Lightning Bolt had split off under a colonel of its own, while White Buffalo continued to recognize the authority of the major general. And even though a major general of the regular army had been appointed to the district, there was no mistaking who people meant when they said "the major general"—that was the commander of White Buffalo. And even though there were many colonels around, if someone said "the colonel," everyone understood that they meant the Lightning Bolt commander, the opponent of the major general who was also trying to get his men into town.

There was only one battalion of the regular army stationed in the town, armed one-to-four, or one rifle for every four men. The militias, on the other hand, were estimated to number around two thousand irregular combatants, if the family members accompanying them were excluded, descending like locusts on the fertile valley where the town was located. They lacked a unified command, to be sure, but they were brave and more experienced fighters, both against the enemy and among themselves.

But the authority figures in the town knew where their strength lay in relation to the militias. They were confident that neither of the militia bands would try to force the issue, in case their opponents linked up with the regular army to put an end to their ambitions to control the town. So they proposed that a three-sided negotiating forum be held between the two militia units with the local administration—including the local headman and the major from the regular army battalion—as the third party.

To enable the negotiations to take place, the local administration authorized each commander to enter the town with an escort of sixty men. In their fear of what might happen, none of the townsfolk left their homes on that fateful day, preferring to catch glimpses of what was going on through gaps in the walls of their houses. You just never knew!

The date, place, and time of the negotiations had already been announced on the notice board that had been erected at the town's only crossroads. On the appointed day two armed units would enter the town from different directions. Still, people doubted whether each side would stick to the agreed conditions. For example, they feared that one side would bring in more troops than the number specified. As the time drew near the whole town fell silent. Indoors, stories circulated about the colonel and the major general. Some said that the colonel was illiterate and a master of the occult; others said that the major general had two wives, one from his own village and one from the family of the sultan who had been overthrown in East Sumatra. But no one had any information about their military skills. In fact there were people who said that neither of them had ever even held a weapon—with the added declaration that anyone versed in occult knowledge had no need of weapons. No one, including the troops under their command, had ever seen either of them. The only exceptions were their personal bodyguards, who formed small, separate units. Both of them were always surrounded by a heavy security presence. All of this was talked about in whispers, with someone even adding that the colonel used to be a pickpocket.

All the conversations stopped when the clock struck the appointed hour. The sound of gunfire rang out. Just one volley. Then silence. The whole town awaited the next move. Then from behind closed doors people started taking peeks at the hill where the headman's office stood, the designated site for the negotiations. Gunfire could be clearly heard from the south, the major general's direction. Then there was a barrage of shots: rat-ta-ta-tat!

Surely they couldn't be facing off against one another right now? With hearts pounding, everyone held their breath.

But then it all went quiet again. The only sound came from the river that divided the town into northern and southern sections, with the hill where negotiations were to take place the defining feature of the north. It had been agreed that each side's troops would head toward the bridge in the middle of town, where the two sides would take up a position on either side, facing each other across the river. Each of the commanders would go forward from here, accompanied by two aides who were permitted to carry pistols.

From the direction of the hill, people could hear the town crier beating the gong and calling on them to come out of their houses and go about their normal business. At first they stepped out hesitantly, glancing left and right in search of assurance. But the sight of their neighbors emboldened them, and in the end everyone had come outside, even if it was only to stand on their verandas, telling the children to remain indoors. No one would have dared climb the hill where the headman's office was—looking toward the bridge was enough to fill them with fright. There, on either side of the river, equal numbers of troops stood guard—fearsome, disheveled, but fully armed, two armies facing off in a militarized zone between two warring states. Some of them had managed to arm themselves with three different weapons: two pistols and a submachine gun or rifle. With a knife as well. Each side had also brought full machine guns. Lightning Bolt had seven, two heavy and five light; White Buffalo had five, three heavy and two light. But most startling of all was White Buffalo's antiaircraft cannon. One of their men was polishing it with his red neckerchief. And everyone was waiting.

Meanwhile, seeing that all was quiet, people started coming from all over to take a look at the negotiation site, till finally the crowd had quite filled the yard in front of the headman's office. Soldiers from the regular army stood guard, so they were prevented from getting too close. But they could hear talk coming from inside—loud, hoarse voices interspersed with the words of their respected elderly headman as he offered advice and attempted to calm the situation with calls for unity in the struggle against the enemy.

According to reports, the discussions proceeded as follows: Before getting to the matter of billets in the town, the headman demanded that each side take firm action against illegal acts, like forcing the local people to hand over supplies, stripping refugees of their possessions in full public view, and especially, taking the law into their own hands—this had resulted in executions of people they suspected with or without good cause of being enemy spies, like convicting someone just because the colors of the enemy's flag—red, white, and blue—showed up in the material used to make his underpants.

The discussions went on a long time.

While the townsfolk stood waiting under trees out in the yard, sheltering from the heat of the sun, the boom of an antiaircraft gun suddenly reverberated across the sky. This was followed by a series of commands to attention, and from up on the hill they could see the troops on either side of the bridge taking up position. But nothing happened. The men who were engaged in the negotiations came outside and looked below. "Maybe the boys are up to something," said the major general with a smile. Then they all went back inside. But the crowd noticed the gloomy expression on the colonel's face—if only he had a gun like that to boost his position in the negotiations!

The negotiations went on and on. They called for food to be delivered, and as the sun sank lower in the west most of the crowd who had come to witness the outcome began to head home, intending to come back after they'd had something to eat. The troops waiting on the bridge had already eaten. The food stalls nearby were cooking rice and serving coffee and sweets.

Evening fell and everything grew calm and peaceful. People became less fearful. The headman would be able to settle them down. There was a feeling of relief in the air, even if it was only the cool of evening that was diffusing the atmosphere.

Suddenly there was the sound of gunfire in the distance, coming from somewhere in the rice fields down in the valley. Shots and more shots. The negotiators came outside and looked toward the valley. The people grew restless.

A long line of troops was making its way along the road that ran through the rice fields. They were heading up from the valley. As far as the eye could see, there were large companies of militiamen advancing on the town.

Whose troops were they? There was no doubt about it; these were the Wild Tiger brigades that were reported to have been on their way. Wild Tiger fighters were known for their courage in the field of battle, but they also had a reputation for looting, and for executing aristocrats they accused of being in league with the enemy.

The troops by the bridge looked up the hill as if in search of information, because from where they stood they couldn't see the new brigades arriving. All the negotiators were giving this new development their full attention. The townsfolk were aware that the situation had changed. The major from the regular army told his aide to go and meet the new troops as the local headman's messenger.

The messenger went to get his motorbike. But before he could start it up, a pair of orderlies from the brigades down in the valley arrived on horseback. As soon as they reached the yard in front of the headman's office they dismounted in style and strode arrogantly through the line of guards, heading straight for the office.

The elderly headman stepped forward without saying a word. The two orderlies saluted him, then handed him a letter. After he read it, he was silent for a moment then spoke in a voice that betrayed no emotion.

"Brothers, the commander of the Wild Tiger brigades demands access to all existing barracks and orders all troops in this region to report to him."

Then he turned and walked away.

For a moment no one knew what to do. Then the colonel and the major general hurried away, accompanied by their two aides. At this, the Wild Tiger orderlies approached the major from the regular army.

The next day, an announcement appeared on the notice board at the crossroads:

All inhabitants are herewith informed that:
From today, the town of A— is the headquarters of the northern front, under the command of the Wild Tiger Division.

A state of war continues to exist. The civilian administration will keep functioning as normal.

All troops in this region must report to the Headquarters of the Wild Tiger Division, located in the Girls' Training School, 3 Pemandangan Street.

From today, in addition to the currency now in circulation, currency issued by the Wild Tiger Division will also be valid.

Price rises will be severely punished (including execution by firing squad).

The normal curfew will continue to apply between the hours of 6 p.m. and 6 a.m.

Beware of enemy spies!

Once Free Always Free!

Issued on 21 November 1947
At the Headquarters of the Wild Tiger Division

signed
Jaga Dolok alias The Machine Gun.

The townsfolk had grown used to proclamations like this, and they were relieved to see it. Not because of what it said, but because rumor had it that the Wild Tiger commander was a fair and honest man. The only malcontents were some criminal types who were disappointed that there hadn't been any fighting, because that would have opened up opportunities for them to play a part in the events, as had happened on several previous occasions.

The Wild Tiger commander himself didn't enter the town officially until some days later, when everyone turned out to greet him. Among the welcoming party were the headman and the major from the regular army. They received the Wild Tiger brigades as victorious heroes returning from the field of battle, and it wasn't long before stories started circulating about their commander's bravery during armed combat. There was no mention of which particular battle it was, but he had one special attribute that attracted everyone's attention and added to the mysterious glow that hung over him like a crown: when he entered the town he was mounted on a small white horse, and everyone noticed that he was barefoot and wearing a ceremonial cloth over one shoulder. Along with this came the news that his trusted aide was a fourteen-year-old deaf-mute!

Where the colonel and the major general had gone wasn't immediately known, but people were saying that the troops they'd brought along on the day of the negotiations had turned out to be the sum total of their units—they were it! But the really extraordinary news was that they were both sworn enemies of the Wild Tiger commander, as a result of perceived unfairness in the division of spoils from the sultanates they'd overthrown after the sultans were found to have connections with the enemy.

According to the story that was going around, a lot of precious stones had been part of the booty, and they'd had trouble finding a fair method of dividing them up. At this point, so the story went, our major general came up with a cunning suggestion: the jewels would be placed on a platter, then they would draw lots to see who would go first in scooping them up in a bowl while blindfolded. They would continue to take turns like this until all the jewels were accounted for. The major general's suggestion was accepted, and the Wild Tiger commander got to go first. But when he was blindfolded, the major general and the colonel grabbed the platter and ran off with it.

This was the story. No one knew if it was true or not, but the reality was that the major general and the colonel didn't show their faces in the town again while the Wild Tiger commander was in control. And he stayed in control until the enemy attacks became more and more widespread and the Wild Tiger brigades had to withdraw into the mountains to wage guerrilla warfare alongside the regular army.

II

Events conspired to bring me into contact with Jaga Dolok, the Wild Tiger commander in the story above. It happened during the time the guerrilla war against the enemy became more intense, after their second general offensive against the Indonesian Republic.

106

After the enemy began to move toward the town in our valley with their motorized brigades, I found myself part of the guerrilla campaign being planned in the mountains, in my role as editor of the local newspaper. During those first days in the mountains, a meeting was organized in one of the villages between representatives of the civilian administration, the regular army, and Jaga Dolok, as the most authoritative representative of the people's militias. Also present was the highest commanding officer of the regular army for the region as a whole, a colonel. One day he had shown up from down south.

Jaga Dolok seemed respectful of the colonel, even though this colonel was an educated man and the militias were usually suspicious of the educated class—even more so in this case, as the colonel was a graduate of the enemy's military academy during the colonial time. Yet there was something about him and his methods that seemed to attract this militia commander. The respect that Jaga Dolok had for him was passed on to his men as well, even though they maintained their disregard for military order and discipline. They confined their salutes to Jaga Dolok, and when the regular army colonel walked past them he would merely smile, as though not expecting any show of respect from them. And the most surprising thing of all was that one day, this regular army colonel turned up in the company of the militia major general and colonel who'd hightailed it when Jaga Dolok had taken over our town.

The regular army colonel divided up the area of military operations between them. At their first meeting, decisions were made about everything that had to do with the division of responsibilities for the guerrilla struggle and administration by the military. The local headman, our elderly doctor, became military governor. All three of them—Jaga Dolok, our major general, and the colonel—pledged allegiance to the decisions that had been taken.

The legal bases of the operation were guaranteed by the successful integration of the regular army and the militias under a single chain of command—this, among other things, was what I wrote in the stenciled newspaper issued by our regional command.

Indeed, during the first week these decisions were in effect, everything went well. The bridges that the enemy had repaired were immediately sabotaged again by the guerrilla bands. The levy imposed on the population in support of the war effort, which mainly took the form of contributions of rice and livestock, went ahead without coercion, even though it represented a heavy burden on the villagers. Every violation of the rules was met with the most severe punishment possible: execution on the spot!

The people were overjoyed with the way things were turning out, and they offered enthusiastic support for every new undertaking. For some months everything went well.

Then the situation changed.

The enemy patrols began to penetrate the upland regions where there were no main roads, even though they couldn't hold any position longer than a few hours because they were cut off from their core units in the towns. After every guerrilla attack they would withdraw to their baseline positions. It was at this stage in the conflict that difficulties began to resurface, and it was precisely at this moment that I had the chance to make direct contact with Jaga Dolok.

It happened like this: One day the enemy took control of a village, only to abandon it again after a guerrilla attack. But as was their practice elsewhere, before they withdrew they set fire to the village. Later, I was able to inspect the burnt-out ruins. Jaga Dolok was also there, conducting an inspection of his own. He was standing in the middle of what remained of the village, flanked by his subordinates. He looked stunned, as though he was trying to absorb the grief of the villagers who sat around in groups near the ruins of their simple village houses. None of them wept, apart from a few old women who were crying over the bodies of children. Several little ones had been shot or had died in the fires that engulfed the places where they'd been hiding from the fighting. Some were caught in the crossfire when they ran out with the men who'd evaded capture and were trying to meet up with the incoming guerrillas. A small number of village men had acted as guides for the enemy, in response to the intimidation they'd been subjected to by the guerrillas; this was all acknowledged in the subsequent investigation. The traitors—three of them—were squatting on the ground under guard, not far from where Jaga Dolok was standing. As I approached, our eyes locked, and he said, "You're the editor of the newspaper, aren't you?"

"Yes," I replied.

"Write this all down," he said, and then he went toward the three traitors. Without warning, he moved the guards aside, kicked one of the prisoners, and then quickly drew his pistol. Then came the sound of a bullet—fired into the ground. The three traitors were witless with fear, looking at Jaga Dolok with transfixed and lifeless eyes. One of them prostrated himself at his feet. Jaga Dolok turned and walked away. The traitors were marched off by their guards.

That afternoon he summoned me and asked me to lead the enquiry. The military prosecutor was a day's travel away, too far off to take charge of the situation himself. I had no experience in this type of investigation, I told Jaga Dolok.

"You are an educated man," he said. "I want you to interrogate them!"

Two of the men claimed the enemy had forced them to act as guides, and the third told how his daughter had been raped by one of the guerrillas.

"Let them go," was all Jaga Dolok said once the enquiry was over. Then he signaled me to follow him.

This would be my first visit to his headquarters, I thought. We headed out of the village and into the open fields.

"Are we going to your headquarters?" I asked.

"No," he replied.

We came to the edge of a valley where I could see a small hut down at the foot of the silent slopes. A thin wisp of smoke rose above it.

"That's where we're going," he said.

Someone was coming up from below to meet us. When he came closer I could see that it was the mute boy who was his aide.

"Don't you have a guard watching the hut?" I asked.

His white horse was grazing nearby.

"No," he replied.

"He doesn't trust anyone," I thought. Then I asked, "Isn't that dangerous?"

Jaga Dolok just smiled in reply. Actually, you couldn't call it a smile, because his face didn't lose its bleak and forbidding look. In fact he looked even grimmer. His skin was dark and his face was covered with the scars of some kind of disease. The breadth of his face belied his small stature. He was still barefoot, and he had the bloodshot eyes of a man who was being hunted—or was it a man who was himself the hunter?

"I'm not afraid of the enemy," he said as we descended by a narrow pathway. The whinnying of his horse echoed around the little valley.

"That horse stands out from a distance, doesn't it?" I said. "The enemy might see it here."

"You mean Sugar? She has magic powers!" he said.

We had arrived in front of the hut, the walls and roof of which were entirely made of thatch. Inside was empty, apart from a mat spread out on the ground. A rucksack lay in one corner. There was a small fireplace with a flame rising out of it. A clay pot stood on top. The light coming in through gaps in the dry thatch made everything clearly visible.

The aide remained outside.

"Sit down," he told me. "She's not back from the river yet, it seems," he went on, as though I knew who "she" was.

"Who?" I asked.

"Maimunah," he replied, standing up to have a look inside the clay pot. "Maimunah. You don't know her. She'll be here in a minute."

I had heard that he kept a woman.

I'd also heard that he had a wife and five children.

Word had it that his family lived in another town, where they'd been taken into custody by the enemy. After holding them for some time, the enemy had sent them back to the village. Who was this Maimunah? Some girl Jaga Dolok had abducted?

From outside came the sound of a woman's voice: "Who's he got with him?" There was no reply. No doubt the mute was using signs of some kind to describe me.

Suddenly an attractive young woman appeared at the door, neatly dressed in simple clothes. "She's so young," I thought, looking at Jaga Dolok with a sense of revulsion. The presence of this woman made the grim atmosphere that radiated from the look in his eyes and his movements all the more noticeable.

She came into the hut carrying a water kettle on a cord strung over her shoulder. "Who's this, dear?" she asked, speaking to Jaga Dolok as a wife would to her husband, with the Malay accent of people from down on the coast. My conversation with him was in the language of the upland people, which he knew even though he wasn't a local.

"This is the man from the newspaper," Jaga Dolok said. "Get us something to eat, would you?"

After that we were silent while she prepared the food—rice, grilled dried fish, and raw chilies.

She didn't join us. "Will she eat later?" I wondered. I almost asked, but held back. We ate in silence.

When we'd finished eating and were rolling cigarettes in dried palm leaves, she took her meal. But it wasn't the rice and fish she'd made for us. Instead, from a dark corner of the hut she brought out a tin plate containing the local dish of coagulated buffalo milk.

"Oh, so that's how it is," I thought.

Jaga Dolok signaled for me to follow him outside.

"This isn't where I live," he said once we were out of the hut.

"Where do you live?" I asked.

"All over," he said.

"So how do you keep in contact with your men?" I asked.

Jaga Dolok pointed toward his young aide, who was sitting on a rock near the hut.

"Do you remember," he went on, "the major general and the colonel who took off in fright when my men entered the town?"

"Yes, they were the ones who were at the meeting a while ago to merge the different commands, weren't they?" I said.

"Oh, yes, that's them," he said. He was silent a moment. Then, all of sudden, "They're waiting for a chance to get back at me!"

"They did something wrong, didn't they?" I was thinking of the story of the jewels they'd got away with.

"Not that," he said. "Maimunah!"

This seemed to let me in on what was really going on. So it had nothing to do with the jewels! There was something here that was more valuable than a few jewels.

But who was stealing whose property in the case of this woman? I wondered. This made it seem as though Maimunah wasn't Jaga Dolok's prisoner, someone he'd forced to go with him.

"So isn't it dangerous to leave Maimunah in an isolated spot like this?" I asked.

"There's always one of my men here," he replied.

"But what good would one man be if a group of them turned up?" I continued, convinced now that his enemy was the major general or the colonel, one of whom was out to rob him of Maimunah, his most treasured possession.

"It would be even more dangerous if I posted a real guard on her," he said. I looked at him in surprise.

"You don't get it, do you? When it comes to action against the enemy, I can trust my men implicitly. And I have no doubts about my bodyguards' loyalty. If I ordered them to kill someone for me none of them would hesitate. But . . ."

"But what?" I said.

"Well . . ."

"And Maimunah herself, what does she think about it?" I asked. "Is she happy with the way things are?"

"She doesn't like it, but she can't go back," he said.

"Go back where?" I asked, as though I was trying to get a confession out of him.

"Back to town, of course," he said.

"So she's the daughter of a . . . ?" I asked.

"Yes," he said. I was quiet for a moment. Then I said, "It's dangerous for her to be left alone here."

"Sugar can tell when there's someone several hundred meters away," Jaga Dolok said. "The wind out in the open fields keeps changing direction, so if there's someone approaching from any direction she can tell. And Maimunah keeps on the move. Sometimes she's in a village."

"Aren't you afraid I'll give your hiding place away?" I asked, realizing that for the first time in our conversation I'd addressed him in a way that made us brothers in arms.

"No, because I'm intending to put Maimunah's fate in your hands," he said evenly. At first I didn't know what to say.

"What do you mean?" I asked once I'd got my voice back.

"It's like this. You should know her background." Then he related his life story. It turned out he wasn't from the upland regions as people thought. He was the son of a stable hand in a horse-riding club down in the city. The members of the club were all Europeans and high-ranking Indonesians during the colonial time, and Maimunah's father was a senior official in the colonial administration, a traitor who'd sided with the Dutch and was executed by Jaga Dolok's own militiamen.

When the revolution broke out, Jaga Dolok had become a brigade commander, even though he knew nothing about military affairs. When he'd first come across Maimunah, she was being held prisoner. Her captors were fighting over her, and Jaga Dolok rescued her.

"I'm not a good man. I've killed plenty of people—traitors, uncooperative prisoners, and men in my unit who've violated the disciplinary code or committed acts of intimidation. On top of that, I've wanted to take revenge on well-off people like Maimunah's father, who almost without exception sided with the enemy, the colonialists, and looked down on the ordinary people. But I've known Maimunah since she was a little girl taking horse-riding lessons. She went away to school, and I didn't see her again till after the revolution broke out. I took my white horse from the stable where my father was a supervisor. He's still there, in fact."

"Have you got a family?"

"Yes," he replied, but offered nothing more. So I kept asking questions.

"Why do you want to hand Maimunah over to me?"

"I want . . . I would like you to marry her," he said, "so other men will leave her alone."

For the next few days I couldn't get this idea out of my head. His final words were fixed in my brain: "You'd make a good husband for her. You're an educated man."

I'd had no intention of getting married, especially under circumstances like these and in such an unexpected way. I'd been more interested in Maimunah as a victim of unpredictable fate than as a person in her own right. What's more, I'd only just become aware of her existence. But what if this was the only way to protect her?

"She's beautiful," I thought, and my mind wandered to other things as well. She'd be a fitting companion once I was working for a big paper in the city!

A week went by, and I still hadn't given him an answer. I didn't see Jaga Dolok the entire time. He was busy organizing guerrilla actions against the enemy out on the main roads.

At times when I was sitting around with nothing to do, I'd find myself thinking I might accept his proposal. But what would

Maimunah think about it? Before this it had never occurred to me to wonder what she might want for herself. Was she still out there in the valley?

The enemy patrols were giving our district a wide berth. All we saw was the occasional reconnaissance plane flying over.

Then I heard that Maimunah had been moved. One of Jaga Dolok's messengers brought me the news. It was at that moment that I decided I would marry her.

But the next day an enemy patrol appeared, a large number of soldiers fanning out in three different directions across the plateau where the guerrillas had their base. I joined one of the militia units as they withdrew to take up an alternative position. Clashes occurred in several places. The biggest of them involved the units commanded by our major general and colonel. Many men belonging to their units were killed. Their situation was so dire that if Jaga Dolok's troops hadn't got there in time to back them up, they would certainly have been wiped out.

When the fighting was over and the enemy withdrew, I saw Jaga Dolok again. At the suggestion of the local people, a buffalo had been slaughtered and a victory celebration was underway. I intercepted him as he moved among the people, to tell him I was ready to go ahead and marry Maimunah as he had asked. But when I spoke the words he said nothing, just kept walking. "Maybe he's changed his mind," I thought. "People are always doing that."

The following day I was intending to go and find his headquarters. But just as I was about to get going—having set up the stencil for the next issue of the newspaper—a messenger turned up with a letter from him. The news came as a shock: Maimunah had been captured by the Dutch!

Without waiting for a reply, the messenger was gone. I didn't know whether to feel sad or relieved. But after I'd thought about it a while, I got the feeling that this was the best outcome for Maimunah, even though it felt as though something beautiful had just slipped through my fingers. What fate would await her in the hands of the enemy? But I wasn't seriously worried. Her father had been a high-ranking official, a weapon against the Indonesian people in the hands of the enemy.

After that the everyday work routine soon stopped me thinking about Maimunah, even though she was still there somewhere in the back of my mind. At times I found myself wondering what she was doing down in the town. I felt sure that the enemy soldiers would have returned her to her family.

The situation kept changing. One day, I heard that Jaga Dolok and the major general had been fighting, and that Jaga Dolok had shot him right through the heart. Not long after that came the news that Jaga Dolok himself had died in battle, during an ambush of the enemy somewhere along the main road.

The war came to an end. At long last full independence was achieved.

Under the changed circumstances I moved back into town. I was offered a position as head of the provincial information office, but I turned it down. I had never wanted to be a civil servant. Instead, I became a journalist with one of the local newspapers.

Life gradually returned to normal. Conditions were becoming more orderly, moving away from the revolutionary atmosphere, although there was quite a lot of political turmoil. It was in my nature to be sensitive to external circumstances, so the more orderly environment meant I was becoming calmer within myself. Had I really lived the life of a guerrilla fighter? I asked myself a few times. But after five years had passed, questions like that faded from my mind.

However, one night I had to attend a reception on behalf of my paper—this was the sort of job that fell to me. It was a lively affair, as was normally the case at that time. People were fond of holding receptions, and attending them as well. As usual on these occasions, I spent most of my time observing people. These affairs attracted a lot of beautiful women, all expensively dressed as though in anticipation of the prosperous times that lay ahead. The overall effect was dazzling.

Suddenly I saw an attractive woman who looked familiar. Where had I seen her before? When was it? Yes, sure enough—it was Maimunah! As though we'd never lost contact, I headed straight for her and greeted her with a brazen "Hello there!"—something I'd never said to a woman before. There was no doubt about it—

she looked at me without surprise, and with no pretense of not knowing me. "Hello!" she said. "How are you?" Her voice sounded completely natural.

"I'm fine," I said evenly. "Good."

A man approached and took her by the arm, leading her in the direction of another group of guests. I turned around and looked vaguely at the crowd absorbed in lively conversation. Was that really Maimunah?

Leaving the reception, I headed off to the office. The traffic on the streets was flowing normally.

The next day I thought again about my unexpected meeting with Maimunah. "How could that possibly have been the old Maimunah?" I wondered. Maybe it was another woman entirely?

But just as in a perfect short story, the answer to the puzzle unfolded of its own accord. One day, an invitation turned up from the local army command to the swearing in of a new battalion commander, a major someone-or-other. When I saw his name, I realized that this major was our old militia colonel! (Not the colonel from the regular army, who had been the commander of the district as a whole.)

Out on the field where the ceremony was held, I got as close to the front as I could and immediately examined the new commander. Yes, it was indeed our old colonel, even though he wasn't easy to recognize in full army uniform.

When I offered him my congratulations at the reception that night, he recognized me right away. Slapping me on the shoulder, he cried out, "It's you! Hey, I'd forgotten all about you! What are you up to? Still doing that writing?"

"Yes, yes," I said, nodding my head and then moving along to let other people shake his hand.

"Stick around, won't you?" said the new major. "We must have a chat about the old days!"

He seemed really happy to see me. Whenever he was left alone he sought me out to talk, and when the reception was over, he still wouldn't let me go. One story after another. Laughing all the time. He really was the friendly type.

"All those stories about the bad things the militias did, three quarters of them were just lies, if not ninety percent of them," he said. "You know yourself what it was like."

He looked at me and laughed.

"Should I tell him about Maimunah?" I wondered.

After a moment's silence, he beat me to it. "Hey brother, do you remember Maimunah? She's married to some bigwig these days.

"Funny how things turn out," he went on with a sigh. "I almost married her myself back then."

For a moment I didn't say anything. Then, just to keep the conversation going, I remarked, "You know, I have no clear memory of anything from those days, apart from that white horse Jaga Dolok used to ride. When I think back on the ups and downs we lived through back then, it's all just a blur of good memories. But that white horse? I wonder what became of her?"

"White horse? Jaga Dolok's white horse?" the new commander said. "Oh, the boys slaughtered it for food."

There was nothing else to talk about. I excused myself with the same words all the other guests had used: "I wish you all the best in your new line of duty."

"Thank you," said the new commander.

Once I was outside, my thoughts settled for a moment on the white horse. But then it was gone for good.

I had to get my report straight to the editors.

III

After my meeting with the new battalion commander, I suddenly found myself bored with my job as a journalist for a regional newspaper. The feeling came over me the very next day, and I soon took the decision to resign and send off a letter to Jakarta, asking about the possibility of a job with one of the national newspapers there. It just so happened that one of my old school friends was the editor-in-chief.

As though it was meant to be, my application was accepted, and it wasn't long before I too was in the capital. From the job I was given, it was obvious that the newspaper was looking to put on new staff as cheaply as possible. I began all over again, right on the bottom rung of the journalistic ladder.

During my first few days in Jakarta I was struck by an interesting fact. I seemed to be running into all my old acquaintances from prewar days through the Japanese occupation and into the revolution, after years of not knowing where any of them were. They weren't proper meetings, just glimpses of people among the crowds on the streets: "Hey, isn't that . . . ? Where do I know him from? A friend from school?" But it was rarely the case that I knew for sure whether it was someone I'd known at school or some other period in my life.

There was only one group of people I met at this time who gave me a sense of continuity with the past, reappearing now as though part of an unbroken sequence of events.

After my arrival in the capital, there were two places I visited on a daily basis. The first was the Housing Office, where I went in search of a room. The second was the busy Senen district, where there was a restaurant called "Loyalty" that for a time became my regular haunt. I don't go there anymore, not since the events of a few weeks ago that form the basis of this part of my story.

There is a connection between the Housing Office and the Loyalty restaurant in Senen, where I met up with many people I'd known during the years of revolution. It was as though there was a direct line that took me from one to the other.

The first time I entered the big waiting room in the Housing Office, I was immediately greeted by a smart-looking young man. I didn't recognize him, but he came straight up and said in a friendly and familiar way, "Oh, you're here in Jakarta now? Are you looking for a house?"

"Just a room," I replied.

"Come with me," he beckoned. "You need to fill out a form at window number nine."

I still had no idea who I was dealing with, but he seemed to be a member of staff. He casually took a form from in front of the clerk at the window, gave it to me, and then disappeared into the back office.

I put my name on the register of applicants and was studying the form when I heard him laughing. Searching him out, I could see him standing by the desk of an elderly man who looked on as the young man gestured like a mute trying to make himself understood.

"What's going on?" I wondered. But a moment later the situation became clear. A few steps in front of him stood a boy who was watching him in a restrained but responsive way. It was the mute, Jaga Dolok's young aide!

I stood up, unaware of what I was doing, and stared through the bars at the window. The mute—his real name was Bonar—seemed to be signaling a reply while looking in my direction. A moment later he leapt up and ran toward me, with a strangled cry that sounded like an animal having its throat cut. All the clerks looked on in surprise as he slapped me on the shoulder, shook my hand, and wrapped me in a tight embrace.

An extended "Mmmmm-mmmmmm-mm" was the only sound to accompany all his hand gestures. He remembered me perfectly. He touched my white shirt, and after patting my chest right on my heart, locked his index fingers tightly together. It was Jaga Dolok and me! Then he moved his hand as though he were writing something, and after pointing to my chest, gave me a thumbs-up. After that he looked me in the face for a moment and then dragged me off with a sign to say he wanted me to go for a drink with him.

At a stall near the Housing Office we were joined by the young man who'd spoken to me when I first arrived. By this time I'd recognized—or perhaps better, had vaguely remembered—him as one of Jaga Dolok's personal bodyguards. Once I'd given him this look of recognition, he smiled and said, "My name's Iskandar! I recognized you right away, and went to find Bonar and tell him I'd seen you. He thought I was only teasing. Have you still got that housing application form? Let me fill it in for you."

The form was still there in my hand. I gave it to him. He asked my full name and other details, writing it all down on the form.

"I'll put it in myself after I go back," Iskandar said.

"Do you work there?" I asked him.

"No," he said as though there was something that needed to be kept quiet. "But these days, what aren't people doing?" I'd heard there was a black market operating in the housing sector before I'd approached the office, but I had no idea I would run into someone I knew who was a part of it. And what was Bonar doing there? How did he get involved in the shady side of the housing market?

This was the meeting that led me to the Loyalty restaurant in Senen. When he'd finished his drink, Iskandar went back to the Housing Office, telling us to wait there at the roadside stall for him. It wasn't long before he was back, this time riding a brand-new red motorbike.

"Come on, get on," he said. "It's all done. Let's go and get something to eat in Senen." Bonar gestured for me to sit behind Iskandar, while he squeezed onto the bike behind me. With a roar of the exhaust, we were off to Senen.

We ate lots of food, and Iskandar forced me to drink some beer—not that I needed forcing. When we'd finished eating, he gave me a lift home, because we'd spent so much time talking. As we parted company in front of the house where I was staying, Iskandar said, "Well, that's it. It's all fixed. But do come and join us sometime at the Loyalty. We're there every night. Also Marius."

"Who's Marius?" I asked.

"Oh yes, that's right. You don't know him. He was a navy commander at Bagansiapiapi during the revolution. He's a great chess player. There's always a game going when we're there."

I like chess, so I said, "I'll see you there."

After Iskandar and Bonar roared off on the red motorbike, I found myself thinking, "Why is he so keen for me to meet Marius?" The name sounded familiar, but Marius was a common name in our home district. Still, it was another week before I went to Senen again. What made me go is that I'd received a housing permit—known at that time by the Dutch term Vergunning Bewoning or VB—for a room on Waru Street. My officemates were amazed at this news, and one of them commented, "You seem to have some special connections." "Yes, I guess I do," I replied, just as surprised myself. It took people years to find somewhere to live, even a garage.

So I wanted to drop in at the Loyalty in Senen to pass on my thanks to Iskandar.

There was a new moon that night, which meant that people had just received their monthly wages. A really big crowd had gathered outside the Grand Cinema, as usually happened when a Malay film was showing. The Loyalty was only ten meters from the Grand, so once I got through the crowd I was almost there.

When I walked in, I could only see two other customers, who were absorbed in a game of chess. I took a seat with my back to the street, facing the chess players. Any two men so fond of chess had to be from my home region, I thought. And I'd already heard that the Loyalty was where all the young unemployed and underemployed men from Sumatra congregated in Jakarta. They'd crossed the straits in droves once the war of independence was over and they'd had to integrate back into society, whether it was through study, black marketeering, working, or just drifting about like these two here.

One of the chess players pulled his head to one side and took a deep drag on his cigarette. He noticed me as he did so, and when he went back to the game he said something to his friend. I was sure they were talking about me. The next moment, the one who'd been concentrating on the board threw down his chess piece and swore. Then he knocked over all the pieces on the board. "Game over," I thought.

"Damn," he said, standing up to stretch his limbs and yawn. Then he sat down again and started to whistle.

"The three of us are all the customers they're going to get tonight," I thought, as I looked around the restaurant. The place itself was a little row house, partially open on three sides to give a good view of the passing crowd.

"You want to play?" the one who'd first noticed me suddenly asked. I nodded, and he gathered up the chess pieces and board and came over to my table.

"I'm Marius," he said, moving his first pawn across the board.

He'd gone for black. His friend came over to watch.

"I've heard about you," I said. But like me, he was clearly keeping his curiosity in check. The game went on.

Then, moving his bishop as he spoke, he asked suddenly, "What's your clan?" in the Batak language of North Sumatra. This made it clear that he knew we were from the same region.

"Situmorang," I said, and he reached across to shake my hand before moving his knight.

"I'm a Simatupang. Watch out for your knight, cousin," he said in the respectful mode traditionally observed by people meeting for the first time in my region. I noticed the ring he was wearing, with its delicate little green stone, and his fine dark fingers. He was dark-skinned, and quite short, but he was well proportioned and there was a real presence about him. His hair was smoothly combed.

"Where have we met before?" he asked as he kept on playing. "Are you from Tarutung?" "No, Samosir," I said, and added, "Iskandar mentioned your name to me."

"Oh, you're the one who got the room." He knocked over his own queen.

"You're good at this," he said, looking toward the street where an old man was approaching the restaurant. He seemed to know him.

When he reached the entrance, the old man stopped and called out, "Simatupang! Could I please have a word with you?"

"There's something going on here," I thought. The way this old man was addressing Marius—by his clan name only—was far too respectful for talking to someone so young. Then the old man spoke again. "Here is the money you asked for."

By this stage, Marius was on his feet. He looked surprised.

"The money you asked for," the old man repeated.

"I didn't tell anyone to ask you for money," Marius said with a seriousness that made it seem as though he wanted to make up for some wrongdoing.

"But you told two of your men to come round to my place and get it from me. They were just there. I told them"—and here the old man's voice changed, taking on a tone of flattery with a provocative edge—"I said I couldn't believe you would have the heart to demand money from a poor low-paid worker like me. Simatupang honors the ways of our ancestors, I told them. He wouldn't do something like that to me." The old man gave Marius a sly look, while Marius himself looked both confused and angry.

"It's all right. I'll take care of it. You go home now," he said. Then there was a sudden change of focus. "Hey, that's him, the punk," Marius cried, rushing outside and grabbing hold of a young man who was looking into the restaurant from the busy street in front.

"Yes, that's them," the old man said to me, watching Marius drag the guy into the restaurant, right up to where the old man was standing.

"Is this the man?" Marius asked him.

"Yes, that's him," he said. "But don't go punishing him. It's enough for me to know that you really do honor the ways of our ancestors. I didn't believe for a moment that you would tell someone to take money off someone like me, when there are so many people around with money to burn."

"Please, I want you to slap his face, right here in front of me," Marius said, gripping the young extortionist by the hand. But the old man hesitated, obviously uneasy with what Marius was demanding.

"That's not necessary. Just tell him that's not the way to behave. Really, that's all I need. You've got to feel some sympathy for young men these days. I understand. I do!" With this, the old man turned to go. But before he could make a move, Marius suddenly punched the young man in the face, knocking him to the ground at the old man's feet. As the victim got to his feet, blood all over his lips, the old man stepped back in shock.

"Come on!" Marius yelled. "Tell this old man you're sorry." At this, the young man apologized, watched by the crowd that had gathered around.

"Beat it! All of you!" Marius barked savagely, and the crowd dispersed. The old man shook Marius's hand and left as well. All the while, Marius's friend was silent. Once the old man was gone and calm was restored to the restaurant, Marius beckoned the young man to come and sit with us.

"You silly fool, using my name in front of him like that," he hissed angrily. "You're a hick! You don't have a clue! I told you to keep my name out of it. That old windbag's a relative of mine, remember? Though I wouldn't give you a cent to keep him in the family." This last remark seemed to be directed to me, because it was followed up with some more information. "He used to be rich.

A top-rank smuggler. But oh-so-pious in church. He made out he was poor. Only ate meat once a month, and even then it was no more than a scrap. Not enough for my cat! What's the point of being rich, if you're going to live like that?"

The young man started crying. Soon he was sobbing, which only served to infuriate Marius even further.

"Crying again, you girl? Do you want me to send you back to Sumatra? Silly fool! You want me to send you off to buy a ticket for tomorrow's boat and take you down to the harbor at Priok like I did with Humala? You want to go back to the village and survive on mud?"

But a moment later he'd settled down and seemed to be deep in thought. I excused myself and set off home, thinking over what I'd just seen. I had an urge to go and see Iskandar and Bonar, the mute, to get some sense of what it all meant. I had the feeling that they were my key to understanding the world I'd just been privy to.

It was clear that Marius was the top gangster in our part of the capital. All the other tough guys seemed to recognize his authority. At least that's what Iskandar told me after I tracked him down. "He'll help you out any time you like. Just tell me if you need anything."

I couldn't work out what it was about Marius that made him so special in the eyes of these young men. I asked Iskandar about it and he said, "He knows how to behave, and he's clever too. He used to be a navy commander in Bagansiapiapi. And now lots of his men from those days are wandering around here in Jakarta."

"What does he do for a job?" I asked.

"Whatever turns up," Iskandar said. "As long as you have your wits about you, you can get by on all sorts of things here. What's more . . ." He seemed to pull back from saying anything else.

I was getting an idea of what they were up to. From here in Senen there was a direct line to the black market in licenses that operated on Gajah Mada Street, and then another line to people like Iskandar in the Housing Office. I'd been a beneficiary myself and I'd seen the power they wielded.

There was a great gulf between their world and the world of everyday life, and I was right on the edge of the abyss between the two.

Iskandar started up his bike, saying, "I'll be off now. If you need a bike, you can always use this one on Sundays. Just let me know, anytime."

"I can't ride a motorbike," I said. "Where's Bonar? Tell him to come round to my place sometime."

In the face of the abyss that yawned before me, the mute Bonar was like a rope bridge that might help me cross over into the dim reaches of memory. I wanted to see him and talk things over.

But it was a long time before I did meet up with him, and even then it was only by chance. Before that I'd only seen him flashing by on the back of Iskandar's red bike. When Iskandar opened up the throttle, he would raise his chin to the wind and look ahead with a wild look in his eyes as though he had hand grenades strapped around his waist, and pass a hand through his hair as though he was waving a machine gun in the air. Just like he used to do!

One night I had an invitation to a birthday party for the daughter of Mr. P., a big entrepreneur from our home region whom I'd known for ages through my work as a journalist. Still, this was the first time I'd been to his house. And I'd never seen the girl whose birthday it was. People said she was a very pretty seventeen-year-old that lots of young men had in their sights.

Once I set eyes on her, I could believe it. And she was friendly too. I can't dance, so while the dancing was underway I had a chance to talk to her.

"I know you," she said. "From your writing, I mean. You write really well. I enjoy all your stories."

I warmed to her straightforward style. There was no pretense at flattery, or just being nice. She brought me a drink and something to eat, leaving all the boys who wanted to dance with her in the lurch.

"Do you like writing?" I asked.

"Oh no," she replied. "I know I don't have any talent for it. But it must be nice to be a good writer. There's so much you can talk about."

When I looked at her in profile there was something about her that aroused my suspicions. I noticed the fan in her hand. She was looking around the room in every direction. Over in one corner near the food and drinks table there was a group of boys and girls squealing with laughter. One of them, with his back to us, seemed to be rather drunk. He was being supported by a few of the boys while another boy was pouring a big bottle of beer into his mouth.

Suddenly he stretched and knocked the bottle away. As it clattered to the floor the laughter increased. The boy slumped against the wall opposite us; it was Bonar, all dressed up in fresh clothes and with a coat and tie to boot. He smiled and stood up again, not really drunk at all. His shirt was wet with beer, and he smoothed it out and looked around him, oblivious to the girls and boys who stood there laughing at him. He seemed to be searching for something, and he was signaling with his hands.

The host's daughter was watching him from where we were standing. She turned to me and said, "That's Bonar, the mute. He's in love with me. Funny, isn't it? But he's an interesting boy. My father has given him a job in our company, as a watchman. He's like part of the household here."

Bonar had spied Roswita, as the birthday girl was called. It seemed she was the one he'd been looking for. He started moving toward us, keeping close to the wall the whole time. Without saying anything, Roswita stood up and casually moved away. The mute kept walking till he was right by me. He just stood there, the contortions of his face radiating a deeply felt sadness. His eyes followed Roswita around the room.

"Mmmm-mmmm-mmmm." The strangled cry coming from his throat seemed to add to the pain he was feeling. He took a flower from the vase on the table in front of me, and without taking his eyes off me, picked the blossom off its stalk and dropped it on the floor.

All around us people were dancing the samba. There were tears in the mute's eyes. I got him to sit down. All at once he calmed down and acted as though nothing had happened, just sat there watching people having fun.

I heard the noise of a motorbike outside and looked out a nearby window. Someone was signaling to me. I couldn't hear what he was saying because the bike's engine was still running, so I went out to see what he wanted.

"Tell Iskandar and the mute to come outside," this stranger said. His tone was rough and commanding, and I wasn't going to argue with him.

"Who should I say it is?" I asked. "And what's it about?"

"I'm the one who knocked Lionheart out," he said. "They've got to come right away. There's combat in Kemiri Street . . . Marius . . ."

I went back inside and got the mute. When he saw the man I'd been talking to, he headed straight for him. Iskandar, who turned out to be at the party as well, was caught up in the dancing. I got hold of him and brought him outside, but the stranger had already left, taking the mute with him.

I told Iskandar what was going on. "Something's up," he said. "Come on, we'll go and find Marius, if he's still around." He was acting as though this were part of his regular routine, but I hadn't a clue what I was doing. All I knew was that I wanted to go with him. I climbed on the bike, and as we roared away from the party, I found myself thinking about the mute, which then led me to Jaga Dolok.

I had some kind of premonition about what was happening.

We were heading for Marius's place. When we got there, it was clear he wasn't home. "The station," Iskandar yelled, and we were off again, heading for Gambir Station.

"What's at Gambir?" I asked.

I thought of Maimunah.

"I think we're too late," Iskandar said.

The white horse.

"Too late for what?" I asked him.

The militiamen's waving red neckerchiefs.

"To see the action," he said.

When we pulled up in front of the station, it was nearly six in the morning. A big crowd of people were waiting to board the express train to Surabaya. Iskandar left the bike leaning on its stand and surveyed the main road, as though expecting to see someone.

There weren't many cars coming into the station by then, because the train was now nearly ready to leave.

Suddenly a little van appeared from Pejambon Road, crossing over and entering the station forecourt. Iskandar ran toward it and I followed. When the van came to a stop, out stepped Marius and three other men. Marius looked at me for a moment, and I could see he was in pain. He was wearing a jacket.

"You two keep a lookout here," said one of Marius's companions. "Give us a signal if anything happens." Then they followed Marius into the station. From where I stood it was clear that Marius was limping. I couldn't work out what was going on, but I didn't dare start asking questions.

"Mr. Marius was hit," said the van driver.

"Hit by what?" I said, though I already knew what he meant.

"It's his leg. It's bad," he went on. "But no one knows what's happened to the mute."

"What's it got to do with him?" Iskandar shot back.

"The other side got him," said the van driver. "The main thing is that Marius is okay. I just hope they leave the mute alone. That's what's worrying me!"

Iskandar looked at me as if ready to explain. I held back from asking anything, but he went ahead and told me anyway. "When something like this happens, Marius usually has a train ticket for Surabaya ready to go. Hopefully he'll get over this soon." Dawn had broken and the express train was leaving. With a sigh of relief Iskandar looked toward the main road, where a police siren was approaching the station.

A few days later there was a report in the paper saying that the mute had been found, shot dead and floating in the river. When I read about it in the city news column, I phoned the home of the entrepreneur Mr. P. to speak to Roswita.

She wasn't home, but I saw her later at the burial, along with her parents and lots of people from our home region. People from all sorts of backgrounds turned up that day to pay their respects. For them, the fact that the mute was someone they shared a homeland with was enough to make them feel they should be part of the funeral procession. I didn't stay long. I couldn't see the open grave for the number of people pressing in around it as the hymns were sung. When the minister began the prayers, I walked away.

I turned around once I was some distance away, and looking back through the crowd of mourners I caught a glimpse of the mute's coffin, covered in flowers.

Translated by Keith Foulcher

SOURCE TEXTS

COMBAT

"Pertempuran." Pts. 1–3. *Siasat* 9, no. 401 (1955): 24–26; 9, no. 404 (1955): 24–27; 9, no. 409 (1955): 24–25, 32.

"Pertempuran." *Pertempuran dan Saldju di Paris: Enam Tjerita Pendek* (Jakarta: Pustaka Rakjat, 1956), 3–46.

THE DJINN

"Djin." *Konfrontasi*, March–April 1955, 3–8.

"Djin." *Pertempuran dan Saldju di Paris*, 80–88.

FONTENAY AUX ROSES

"Angelique: Kenangkenangan seorang Pahlawan." *Siasat* 8, no. 381 (1954): 23, 26–27.

"Fontenay aux Roses." *Pertempuran dan Saldju di Paris*, 66–79.

THE INTERNATIONAL TRAIN

"Kereta Api Internasional." *Tjerita*, March 1958, 10–11, 13.

"Kereta Api Internasional." *Pangeran: Kumpulan Tjerita-Pendek* (Bandung: Penerbit Kiwari, 1963), 44–60.

A JUNIOR DIPLOMAT

"Diplomat Muda." *Mimbar Indonesia* 8, no. 10 (1954): 9–10.

"Diplomat Muda." *Danau Toba: Sekumpulan Cerita Pendek* (Jakarta: Pustaka Jaya, 1981), 18–25.

THE LAST SUPPER

"Perjamuan Kudus." *Danau Toba*, 5–17.

MOTHER GOES TO HEAVEN

"Ibu Pergi Kesorga." *Duta Suasana* 4, no. 18 (1955).

"Ibu Pergi Kesorga." *Konfrontasi*, March–April 1955, 9–15.

"Ibu Pergi Kesorga." *Pertempuran dan Saldju di Paris*, 89–99.

OLD TIGER

"Harimau Tua." *Siasat* 8, no. 370 (1954): 24, 27.

"Harimau Tua." *Pertempuran dan Saldju di Paris*, 47–53.

SNOW IN PARIS

"Saldju," *Siasat* 8, no. 350 (1954): 23, 25.

"Saldju di Paris," *Pertempuran dan Saldju di Paris*, 54–65.

About the Author
and Translators

Author

SITOR SITUMORANG was born on October 2, 1924, in the village of Harian Boho, in a small valley at the foot of the mountain Pusuk Buhit, on the western side of Lake Toba, facing the island of Samosir. After spending his early years immersed in Batak culture, he was sent away at the age of seven to be educated in Dutch-medium schools in Balige, Sibolga, Tarutung, and Jakarta. His education came to an end when the Japanese invaded Indonesia in 1942. During the Japanese occupation he worked in local government offices, read widely in European literature, and entered journalism. His first marriage, in March 1944, produced four sons and three daughters.

After World War II, Sitor became widely known for his reporting on the Indonesian revolution against the Dutch, often from Yogyakarta, capital of the new Republic. He was imprisoned by the Dutch for several months in late 1948. Following the revolution, he lived in the Netherlands from 1950 to 1951 at the invitation of the Dutch government, and from 1952 to 1953 lived in Paris, where he worked part-time at the Indonesian Embassy. Sitor began writing poetry in 1948 and is considered a member of Indonesia's literary modernist "Generation of 1945." Throughout his life he was a highly productive and very visible writer, publishing ten volumes of poetry and a number of larger anthologies, three volumes of short stories, and one collection of plays.

Sitor joined the Indonesian National Party in 1953 and became a vigorous spokesperson on the nature of national culture. He was a lecturer at the National Film Academy and studied film at the University of California (1956–57). At various times, Sitor represented the artistic community as a member of the National Assembly, the National Planning Assembly, the Emergency People's Consultative Council, and the Consultative Body for the Assessment of Higher Education. He was chairman of the pro-Sukarno Institute of National Culture from 1959 to 1965 and, following Suharto's accession to power, was imprisoned for seven years as a political dissident.

After regaining his freedom in 1976, he spent long periods abroad. He and his second wife, with whom he had one son, lived in The Hague (1982–90), Islamabad (1991), and Paris (1995–99). Nevertheless, even then he still remained actively involved in Indonesian cultural affairs, and as the son of a senior Batak chief, he regularly returned to Indonesia to fulfill various ritual duties in North Sumatra. He also wrote a number of books on Batak regional culture and history.

Sitor Situmorang died in the Netherlands on December 20, 2014, and was buried in Harian Boho on January 1, 2015.

The Indonesian critic Pamasuk Eneste has written, "Sitor's stories deal with humanity and its problems. He writes about loneliness, love, loss, travel, alienation. . . . He is a poet and this shows in everything he writes."*

TRANSLATORS

HARRY AVELING holds the degrees of Doctor of Philosophy in Malay Studies from the National University of Singapore, and Doctor of Creative Arts in Creative Writing from the University of Technology, Sydney. He is an honorary full professor in the Department of Translation and Interpreting Studies, Monash University, Melbourne, Australia. His recent publications include translations of *Pilgrimage* by Isa Kamari (Singapore: Ethos Books, 2016), *Kill the Radio* by Dorothea Rosa Herliany (3rd printing; Yogyakarta: MataAngin, 2017), and *Why the Sea Is Full of Salt and Other Vietnamese Foktales* by Minh Tran Huy (Chiang Mai: Silkworm Books, 2017). A collection of essays on translation and

---

* Pamusuk Eneste, "Catatan Editor," *Sitor Situmorang: Salju di Paris* (Jakarta: Grasindo, 1994), viii–ix.

Indonesian/Malay literature is forthcoming from the National University of Malaysia Press.

KEITH FOULCHER has written extensively on modern Indonesian literature and cultural history, especially of the late colonial and early independence periods. He is also an experienced translator of Indonesian and has published translations of Indonesian poetry and short fiction. His most recent publication is *Indonesian Notebook: A Sourcebook on Richard Wright and the Bandung Conference* (with Brian Russell Roberts; Duke University Press, 2016). He is also editor, with Mikihiro Moriyama and Manneke Budiman, of *Words in Motion: Language and Discourse in Post-New Order Indonesia* (National University of Singapore Press, 2012), and, with Tony Day, of *Clearing a Space: Postcolonial Readings of Modern Indonesian Literature* (KITLV Press, 2002). He is an honorary associate of the Department of Indonesian Studies at the University of Sydney.

BRIAN RUSSELL ROBERTS is an associate professor of English and coordinator of the American Studies Program at Brigham Young University (Provo, Utah), where his research focuses on US and broader American cultures in transnational contexts, with particular emphasis on Indonesian intersections and questions of archipelagoes and oceans. With Michelle Ann Stephens, he is editor of *Archipelagic American Studies* (Duke University Press, 2017). In 2015 he was a Fulbright Senior Scholar at Universitas

Sebelas Maret in Solo, Indonesia. His prior work in translation includes collaboration with Keith Foulcher on *Indonesian Notebook*, preparing English-language versions of Indonesian-language essays, lectures, and articles related to Richard Wright's Indonesian travels.